First edition independently printed 2023.
This edition printed 2024 by Pope Lick Press.

DEREK HEATH

DARK NIGHTS

STORIES

POPE LICK PRESS
2024

CONTENTS

MY
SAINT
OF
THE
MANGROVES

1995
Levy County, South Florida

A bloated sun pressed the pads of its fingers to the back of his neck, extracting plump beads of sweat from his flesh as he watched the river. Thick, white tree roots arched violently from a crystal-green stream of saline and silt, a thin shell of clear glass; below, the sediment clustered around the trees' root systems was an abundant brown fog.

Near the riverbank, small puffs of sand erupted and dissipated as something moved through the murky seabed. He was distracted by the blossoming explosions for a moment and caught a glimpse of red, salt-encrusted shell: the sometimes-drifting, sometimes-scuttling back of a horseshoe crab.

Andy Holley scribbled frantically in his notepad and returned his attention to the pair of juvenile lemon sharks playing in the tunnels and caves of a gargantuan nest of mangrove roots. The trees were so plentiful along this stretch of river that they formed an antediluvian labyrinth of green and white, and though none of the trees were taller than eighteen or twenty feet, their branches were so perverse and full that everything around them seemed smaller. The juveniles had spent most of the day among the roots of a tall tree, the opposite side of the river to Andy's hiding place; he recognised the first pup as a shark that had passed him in a group of five or six the day before, but the second was new.

The woman who had led him here, a dark-skinned scout who knew the land better than anybody else he'd encountered and seemed to understand the benefit of his observations – more so, perhaps, than the suits reluctantly funding him – had advised him not to name the pups. The mangal was a hungry place, she had said, and to grow attached to any of the fauna was as foolish as developing feelings for a farmyard pig.

He had joked that he hadn't grown attached to anything for a long time.

Andy's eyes peeled upward, tracking the oozing, white ball of the sun as it rolled slowly over his head. His scrawny arms and legs were bare. His shorts were damp with sweat and it lay across his back like a tight, uncomfortable gauze. Some of his notes were smudged where salty moisture had dropped from his thick, sandy hair; two or three days in, he had taken to writing in pencil.

15:30. Two lemons play in the same root system where, yesterday, a school of F. gar came to feed on snook. One pup exhibits the same distinctive markings as #44: three long scars across its nose; a deep notch in its fin. I have designated the second Pup #50: darker gold-brown back, smudge of black on its belly.

He snapped the book shut and looked up again. Crisp ribbons of cloud framed the edges of a languid sky. Christ, he was exhausted. He had come back at dawn and taken only a twenty-minute walk since settling into his hidey-hole; his legs burned from sitting all day and his eyelids threatened relentlessly to roll forward. He would take tomorrow off, he decided; leave this little offshoot of the Suwannee to observe itself for a few hours.

What else had the scout said? About the rain? She had tried at first to warn him against staying out here in it, but when he'd insisted that the biome's dependency on the weather was a vital part of his research, she had seemed to understand. Grimly, she had told him… oh, what had she said?

Down the river, a gar darted playfully through clouds of silt, snapping its jaws around smaller fish and plucking them from the water. On the bank, a pair of male fiddler crabs fought, clicking their obscenely oversized, yellow left claws in a crude dance for the attention of a nearby female. Andy caught a flash of neon fluorescence near the surface, a little closer to him: the fin of a schoolmaster, its silvery scales shimmering as it fluttered in a mad dash for the other side of the river. He was wary of the slow movements of a thick, dull-grey cottonmouth snake in the branches above him, but it was focused on its prey: a twittering green anole lizard, oblivious to the predator as it made twitchy, jerking movements from leaf to leaf.

The river teemed with life, and even after so long he was enamoured with it.

He gazed into the crystalline surface of the river again and watched as the lemon sharks ventured into open water. A knot of mangroves in the middle of the river formed an island of sorts and he watched as the pups swam eagerly around it, grazing the bowed roots with blunt, brown noses. Black eyes flashed in the sunlight as they bumped and snapped at each other, short bodies making quick work of the water, soft fins slicing easily through it.

16:00. Pups #44 and #50 emerge from their
sheltered playground and perform for me in open water.
They seem uninterested in feeding and ignore small schools
of grunts and grey snappers.

Above his head, a branch shuddered as the
cottonmouth lunged forward, its jaws opening wide to
funnel the anole inside. The lizard saw a flash of
fangs—too late—and wriggled back, retreating from
the throat of the monster so that by the time the snake's
lips had closed it was only its head that disappeared.
The snake bit down, hard, and opening its mouth
sucked inwards; convulsing one last time, the anole
vanished.

Don't look into its mouth, the scout had said. That
was it. When it rains, don't look.

Andy leant back and watched the cottonmouth for a
while, marvelling at the brown knots of pattern-work
across its back as it coiled its body around a thick
branch and dragged itself away. Its movements were
almost hypnotic, and the heat bloomed around him in
thick, sticky clouds. Wiping his eyes, Andy exhaled
quietly and shifted his weight onto his butt. Tucking
the notepad into his shirt pocket, he looked left and
right along the river and scratched the back of his head.

The smell of petrichor and mosquito spray was less overwhelming than it had been; almost soothing now, soporific…

He looked toward the 'mouth' of the mangrove. Beyond a spray of greenery on either side, the ocean was a distant gullet of blue and green sprayed with fiery flecks of sunlight.

Listen to me, she had said. When it rains, don't look.

The river was alive, almost electric with life. On the opposite bank, a pink-feathered spoonbill ducked its head repeatedly into the wet sand and drew small insects into its throat; the pair of lemon sharks he'd been watching had skittered off into a deeper part of the river, but a third had swum into their woody natural playpen and lay resting in a shallow cloud of silt. He heard the rattle of a crocodile's throat, somewhere unseen, and all around the ever-present chirruping of cane toads. Clusters of silvery shapes danced elegantly through the green water and he spotted a mangrove crab lifting itself gently off of an underwater root and

(you could take a nap)

floating up to attach itself to a softly drifting leaf. He

(just for a minute)

was tired. Reluctantly, he allowed his eyelids to press forward, nodding his

(just)

head forward and falling asleep in the hot, hot sun.

Andy Holley awoke to the dull sting of a single raindrop on the top of his head. He reeled from it and his skull knocked the branch behind him with a heady thunk. He shivered; the air had turned cool and thick with dew. Blinking, he looked around him; in the burnt orange of a steadily approaching dusk, the river was eerie and still.

Too still, he thought.

It could only have been an hour or two. And even in the depths of night, the wildlife here was just as varied and colourful and loud; even the croaking of frogs had ceased. He leant forward cautiously, gazing into the water. Completely still, splashed with patches of moonlight. There was no movement. No life. He scoured the bank for egrets or spoonbills and saw nothing at all. The soft rain that fell was dashed with amber sparks of refracted sunlight and fell with the flitting, darting sporadicity of pyre ashes.

Off to his left, the long, low splash of something moving through the river. He turned his head slowly, as if afraid the creaking of the bones in his neck might give away his position. His eyes drifted along the bank. He saw it.

Sixty or seventy feet from him, something waded through the low water, dragging long legs behind it and vanishing into the shadows at the edge of his vision.

He blinked again; it was gone.

(when it rains, don't)

But for just a moment, it had been there.

And it had scared away every other living thing.

He thought of Tanya as he adjusted his position in the perch, his mind drifting inescapably to a place he seldom visited; when he did, it was often physically disabling, and sent him spiralling into a depression which could last for hours or weeks. Nonetheless he found himself staring into the river and seeing only the crystal blue-green of her eyes, each tainted with central heterochromia so that the irises blazed with bright gold sparks..

He had never been able to understand why she had left, but he knew now that the reason hardly mattered. There was nothing he'd have been able to do about it, whatever it was. She was decisive, headstrong; once she had elected to leave, there was no choice.

There was certainly nothing he could do now, he thought, shifting his weight again and looking toward the Gulf of Mexico. He wondered why the scout had told him not to; it was beautiful, especially in the rain. Spangles of light danced on the surface of the ocean, waning in the fading sunlight. His legs ached and he longed to move. Perhaps he ought to walk back to camp.

He gathered his notes quickly, tucking a pair of Zeiss West binoculars into his knapsack with his books and pencil. Awkwardly he fumbled his way out of the hide and onto the ground, his boots landing in soft earth.

The river was eerily quiet, save for the dull patter of rain, but as he walked back in the direction of the village he noticed flashes of life on the banks, traces of creatures hiding in the roots and folded into scattered leaves.

A sudden flash of lightning, followed momentarily by a deep roar of thunder. Andy froze. Immediately the rain hardened, smacking the ground around him and forming a deafening wall of percussion. Andy squinted forward, raised a hand to his brow. Something shrieked, way off in the grey. Instinctively he turned toward the sound.

His eyes fell upon the mouth of the river, a ragged scar between lilting trunks that opened onto the great red wound of the sea. The shriek was that of an animal; he saw none. His clothes were soaked already and clung to him with a heavy oppressiveness; he was shivering, he realised, his whole body trembling uncontrollably with the sudden cold. The mouth of the Suwannee was a cavern of dull grey in a landscape increasingly smeared with it; he could see nothing at all, save for the fading silhouettes of the trees.

Lightning washed the sky with white and his eyes widened in horror.

The thing stood knee-high in the churning froth at

the very end of the river. Absurdly, Andy's first thought was that this was impossible, since the water there was deep enough that he'd have to tread quite energetically to stay afloat.

His second thought

(fear)

was that the figure was watching him back.

In that frantic half-second he saw that it was the approximate size and shape of a man, with an abnormal, hooked growth protruding from its left temple. Its arms hung limply on either side of a malnourished body, misshapen around the ribs and waist by some bulky kind of clothing. Its eyes were tiny, white points of light; its mouth was open and grinning and the electric fire of the sky flashed off its teeth.

In the next second, it was gone. The long, low roar of a thundercloud preceded another clap of rain, a curtain of it that fell all at once before smacking the ground and shattering. Andy swallowed.

When the lightning came again, there was no silhouette. No figure.

Andy turned back toward camp and ran.

Rain pelted the tent roof for most of the night and, after a brief hiatus shortly after midnight – during which Andy finally managed to fall asleep – continued well into the morning. Though his sleep was precarious and regularly disturbed, he was physically exhausted and took advantage of the poor weather to neglect his regular schedule and sleep into the day.

He dreamed of Tanya. As beautiful as the day they'd met, her lips moving slowly, forming vague shapes as she spoke to him across a candlelit dinner table. The words were a haze. Something about the spare room in the apartment. Shouldn't they make use of it? What about a nursery? she said. A hint. Another that he hadn't picked up on. Had there been more, in the days – weeks – before she'd left?

She snapped. Andy, are you listening? Where are you?

A pink ribbon of flesh: her arm darting across the table, her palm smacking his cheek. At once he seemed to wake up, eyes snapping to her face. Pain spreading across his jaw. Not the hardest she'd hit him, but somehow it hurt just the same.

He said, Why? and she smiled sickly at him.

Slowly, she opened her mouth.

It fell wide, slack. Her tongue weighing down her lower jaw, pushing, pressing it down to her chest – then there was a snap! and her maw dislocated like a snake's. Skin stretching, saliva starting to dribble over her chin in gluey strings. No, not saliva…

River-water gushed from her throat and cascaded onto the tablecloth, extinguishing the candle with a splash. Water everywhere. Fully aware that he was dreaming but unable to wake himself, to escape, Andy was suddenly engulfed in the saline and weakly paddling, useless against the rushing current. He tumbled, over and over, head smacking a thick knot of bone—

He clawed desperately and grabbed the mangrove roots, his whole body ripped in one direction as the river screamed past him. He looked up, toward the mouth of the river – no longer Tanya's broken jaw but the visceral rupture between earth and sea that exploded into the Gulf of Mexico.

It was all dead. Everything. Shark pups lay bloody in the water, their bodies caught in spindly white roots and flopping uselessly as the river tugged at them. The leathery hide of an American crocodile lay shredded and torn on the bank.

The mouth of the river was grinning at him. Frothing between ragged, watery teeth. His arm slipped and he was thrown back into the water; blooms of red filled the froth and foam around him and he realised his skull was split open, bleeding fast. He flung his arms out to grab for something solid, anything, but all he found were the slippery bodies of fish and eels, more and more of them as he tumbled away from the grinning maw of the river. Tanya's voice:

And what if I left, Andy? Would you listen, then?

The wall of bodies was so thick that he had stopped moving, and now he bobbed uselessly among them, the current pushing him one way and the spongy flesh of thousands of slaughtered shark pups pressing him another.

You always were too busy, Andy, with your research, and your funding, and those god-damned notebooks…

Thrashing madly in the water he swallowed salt, spat, gasped, looked toward the Gulf. The mouth of the river yawed open, a tongue of saltwater lapping at the banks.

If you'd just listen to me, Andy, I wouldn't have to leave you, would I?

It was chewing at itself, he realised, smashing its teeth into the back of its throat, crashing toward him, opening wide – wide – wider—

You just never listen.

Andy screamed as the river closed over him, its gaping maw sucking him in. A massive wave of cold propelled him into the back of its mouth and he and a wave of rubbery carcasses fell down into the dark together.

It was early evening when Andy left the tent. The sky had calmed, and banks of pink and purple curled around the edges of the earth as a fat white sun began to sink into the horizon. The low buzzing of an army of bullfrogs ebbed and waned, a crackling thrum of electricity quietly riding their throats. Andy looked toward the nearest village, little more from here than a ribbon of greasy gas lights, pulsing in the centres of silhouetted buildings and shacks like steadily beating hearts. He turned toward the river.

The scout who had led him to his perch in the mangal stood in the shadows barely six feet ahead of him, her eyes bright and anguished. Her dark skin shone with sweat.

"You've seen it," she said.

"What?" Andy croaked.

"The spirit with the bright white eyes," she whispered. "Santa Muerte."

Andy shook his head. Swallowed. "I don't know what you mean."

She stepped forward suddenly, grabbed his wrist. Her fingers curled tightly into his flesh and she spoke desperately, urgently: "You must leave. You must not return to the river. Not now you have seen the spirit's face."

"I didn't see anything," Andy insisted, shaking her off. "It was raining…"

"You must leave," she snapped. "Now!"

"No," he said, pushing past her. "Leave me alone."

Rough hands on his arms. Gripping tight, yanking him back.

Andy stumbled. Anger peeled across his skull, blinding, and he wheeled around. "Leave me alone!" he snapped through gritted teeth.

He swiped with one arm in an attempt to get her claws off him. She clung to him like a leech, digging her nails into his biceps through his shirt. "Listen to me!"

"Get off!" he yelled. "Get off, madwoman!"

He batted at her arm and her grip loosened; he took advantage of the moment and yanked his elbow upward, out of her grip. It connected with something firm; a sick, wet crack filled his senses and the scout's head tipped back.

She crumpled.

"Oh, god," Andy whispered. The woman drew in an awful breath and her eyes rolled up in her head; she swayed back as if falling through a thick sludge.

Andy saw the root before it impaled her skull but he was too slow to stop her sinking onto it. An awful, sucking whisper as it plunged into the back of her head, glancing across bone and thrusting up through the soft flesh of her eye-socket, barely missing her eye. Blood sprayed the dirt around them. Her body twitched once. Twice.

"Oh, Christ, oh god…"

He sunk to his knees, fumbling desperately for the woman's throat to feel for a pulse. He jammed the pads of his fingers against her carotid artery and waited. She had stopped convulsing, stopped moving entirely.

Nothing.

"No… no, no, no," he wailed, "no, no…"

Movement. From the direction of the village. Crack of a branch. And a voice: low, rumbling. Another. Two men.

(hunters?)

Not far from here. Panic lilted through his blood, sharp needles of it coursing through his whole body like the juddering thrill of an electric shock.

He stood, staggered back. No, couldn't leave her here. Not so close to the tent. If they found one, they'd find the other. He lurched forward, hooked his hands into her armpits and strained to lift her. Nothing. Heavy, stiff body. She flopped back into the earth and he grunted. Arms tired, useless. No choice but to leave her. Run.

He stumbled back. Second voice again: South African accent. Closer.

Run!

Andy ran.

Raining again. Heavy footsteps in the dirt; thick, wet muck sucking at his ankles. Slogging movements. River running past him. Plump drops of moisture bursting apart like shot as they mashed his head. Eyes on the river. A yell. His imagination? Or—

Root smashing his shin, foot caught. Tumbling over.

Andy yelped as he collapsed into the sand, wet gobs spattering his face. Somewhere close by, the low rumble of a Florida panther's gut seeped into the haze of the air. The river chirruped and croaked all around him. Scrambling awkwardly onto his knees, he unhooked his ankle from the mangrove root and winced at the pain. Sprained, at least. He looked up through the wet mist of the rain and watched as the sky split into gold-purple ribbons. For a moment he had a vague memory of his dream: he felt the sting of the slap, the dreadful awe as Tanya's mouth opened and the river poured out…

The river. The rain.

He stood, moaning in agony as his ankle twisted beneath him. His body sagged and he lurched forward, following the stippling sound of the stream. The water glittered gold in the fading daylight and dark shapes moved beneath the surface. A pair of shark pups, dancing for him, one with a murky brown back and the other with a notch in its fin. They batted heads and disappeared into the sunken roots of an overhanging tree as he looked past them.

The mouth of the river was open wide and its tongue stood upright, a grey silhouette in the vague shape of a man. Andy felt cold swell around his ankle and drew in a sharp, relieved breath as the pain sunk away.

Another step and he was in the river, felt it pushing and pulling at his legs.

Before him, the figure with the swollen head raised a beckoning hand

(come)

and blinked its white-point eyes, almost patiently.

Santa Muerte.

Desperate shards of sunlight on the horizon threw a last cascade of white into the air and for a moment the figure was illuminated: it was translucent, Andy saw, its body formed of layers and layers of drizzling rain, slices and sparks of white dashing the shifting grey cloud of its stomach and arms. Sunlight beamed off the back of the thing's head and Andy understood. A golden halo of light spread around its face and he fell to his knees in the water, let it crash around his waist as the rain above grew hard and heavy and sprayed the surface of the river with shrapnel.

Shouts behind him. The hunters approaching, tracking his footprints in the bog. A sharp whistle in the dark. No hope. No hope…

"I'm sorry," he whispered.

The mouth of the river bled with sunlight and the hazy figure looked kindly upon him, its eyes blazing white as the halo round its head split into tendrils. It still beckoned, still gestured for Andy to come forward, curling its fingers almost desperately now.

Andy raised an arm and nodded.

The spirit flickered and disappeared. Andy Holley opened his mouth to speak, but no words came. He squinted into the ever-thickening rain and saw nothing. Trying to stand, his ankle gave out and he fell on his back, suspended for a moment on the surface of the water.

The spirit looked down upon him, its silhouetted head malformed and terrible. The crooked horn protruding from its temple was a spear of grey that crackled with electricity; its whole body throbbed with death.

(should have listened)

"I'm sorry," Andy moaned, but she could no longer hear him.

(listened should have listened should have)

Gently, she pressed her thumbs into his eyes and pushed his head under the water.

PERIODS

OF

GLOOM

Night air slipped into the cell through a tiny crack between two grey stones; with it a whisper of hope. A voice that had called to the boy most nights since his arrival, and one whose voice grew sweeter with every passing moment. The whistle of the wind, the soft beating of bats' wings as they fluttered about the outer walls, the rasp of the trees lining the border: the voice of *outside*.

Renfield lay upon a flat, uncomfortable bed, his hands knotted together on his stomach, his wide, buggy eyes fixed on the dull flags of the ceiling above him. His hair was thick and black and tangled, greasy enough without access to hot water or shampoo that he could almost slick it back as though oiled. He was a wiry, striated sort of boy, his body scrawny like an arachnid's but thick at the joints with bunches of tight, packed muscle. His feet were bare; a pair of canvas shoes lay empty somewhere else in the building, taken from him with the rest of his belongings. He wore only a damp grey shirt and baggy linen trousers; not even suspenders to keep them up. They didn't trust him with *things*.

The cell was small, and though they called this place an asylum there were no padded walls – nor, in fact, any doctors, though he was regularly assured that the beatings administered by various wardens and officers alike were medicine enough to cure him – and though he could squint through the crack between the bricks if he hunched over a little, it only afforded Renfield a slight, angular view upon the border of Transylvania. There was no window of any kind, and without this crack he would not have known that he was still in the country. Or alive. He had surmised that the outer wall of the cell pointed east, for if he looked through this crack in the morning the ragged horizon blazed with gold and amber; this was about the only period of the day when the sky was alight, and the rest of the time the landscape offered to him was dull and mournful, silhouetted mountains swallowed by thick blankets of fog, the castle building in the distance little more than a point of black smudged by the dusty air.

As he laid here now, malnourished and bored to the point of exhaustion, Renfield thought of the world outside. There was little else to do. He flexed his bony toes in the bed, imagining the sensation of soft, spongy dirt between them. Drew an angular knee up to his chest and extended his leg slowly – slowly – keeping his eyes on the dull grey ceiling as, in his mind, he took the first step up a steep and sunlit hillside. As his leg straightened completely the bare sole of his foot sunk into a carpet of moss, cool and crawling with tiny creatures that immediately began to crawl up his heel. He brought up the other leg, extended it as he had the first, and when his foot met the ground he quivered at the intense pleasure of the feeling: soft, earthen ground, not the hard stone upon which he had grown so accustomed to walking. The cool, wet body of a slug bulged beneath his big toe, popped as he put pressure on the leg. He giggled, flashing his teeth in the dark.

Then he was running, scrambling madly up the hill, mosquitoes and moths flitting about him as he pressed into a thick knot of trees, dashing toward the sun as it crawled fat and bloated across a sky painted in maddening strokes of red and pink.

He laughed, his legs wheeling frantically in the bed. He could smell the nectar of the plants around him, the soft scent of the morning on the breeze, hear the rustle of the trees. He was free, finally free, and he would never stop running again for as long as he was alive; there was so much *life* out here, and he would embrace it all. His laughter grew in volume, twisting his cracked lips into an awful, gurning snarl, a dehydrated tongue lapping his teeth as he cackled. He was free – loose – *human*—

"Quiet!" came a hissing voice through the wall beside him. "D'you want the warden to come down here again, you blessed idiot?"

Renfield's legs crumbled flat onto the bed and he sunk back into the dark pit of his life, exhaling a shallow, whistling breath that made his throat rattle. The pregnant belly of his imagination was punctured immediately and from its ruptured, vacuous sac oozed the lifeblood of his optimism, pooling uselessly on the floor where it shrieked, convulsed, and died. The scent of nectar and morning dew was replaced by the faint stink of forcemeat; the warden had brought his dinner an hour or two before, and Renfield had left the damp sludge that they dared to call *impletata* beneath the crack in the wall that served as his only window. It lay there now in a splintered wooden bowl, a dully-glinting spoon thrust into its gut. Slowly rotting.

The meal would be more valuable to him in the morning.

Somewhere in the building – it would have been impossible to pinpoint where exactly – a light was extinguished, and the cell was plunged into absolute darkness. Renfield lay silently in his bed and stared into the pitch void of the ceiling. In his early teenage years the boy had run away from his mother, a drunkard and a bully who had left him as bruised and tender as the mush in the wooden bowl he had left to decompose; most nights now, the young man dreamed of running away again. The wardens' punishments were far more severe than his mother's had ever been;

if he stayed too much longer in this madhouse he would likely end up in a heap on the floor, his neck broken, his face caved in. Worse was certainly possible.

Beside him, a tiny crack of silver moonlight bled through the crack in the wall, a cruelly-grinning smile in the stonework.

When he awoke two flies had gathered on the gently-decaying eggplant. The boy rolled onto his side, blinking a crust of sleep from his weary eyes, and watched as a third insect buzzed softly in through the crack in the wall and landed on the lip of the wooden bowl.

Renfield licked his lips and glanced toward the fourth wall of the cell, a wall of iron bars that separated him from the tiny room and the stone corridor outside. A tall metal pail in the corner of the cell trembled softly as men and women awoke all through the madhouse; all at once, the screaming began.

Cautiously, the boy swung his legs out of the bed and pressed his bare feet to the floor. His gaze returned to the abandoned meal by the wall and he leant forward, gently tilting his weight off the bed and sinking into a crouch, then reaching forward and planting both hands on the stone. Fingers crooked, he paused there for a beat like a cat ready to pounce; his eyes were fused to the wooden bowl, and as the three flies darted erratically about the half-rotten forcemeat and fruit his gaze flickered left-to-right, up, down and everywhere. He crouched that way for a full two minutes or so, greasy black hair in his eyes, watching the wrinkled black backs of the insects as they flitted oblivious to him.

And then he pounced.

His arms were lithe and snapped forward like pincers; immediately his right hand shot out and closed around the first of the flies in a tight fist, crushing the poor thing in less than a fraction of a second. Even before his fist had clamped shut his eyes had fixed upon the second fly, which immediately darted away from the bowl – not immediately enough. His thumb and index finger pinched its plump, black body in the stale air just inches from the dish.

There was a loud *clock* as his teeth slammed together, his jaws closing violently.

The third fly batted its body anxiously against the walls of his mouth, flitting from the back of one tooth to another, darting under his tongue then buzzing furiously free of it and propelling itself up to the roof of his mouth.

Renfield swallowed.

Still poised like an animal over the bowl, he closed his eyes and enjoyed the sensation of the living, wriggling thing slipping down his throat. The buzzing followed it all the way down and he was electrified, its life-force transferred instantly to him. The feeling was immensely pleasing and his whole body trembled, just once, all the hairs on his sinuous arms standing on end.

Opening his eyes, he pinched gently and crushed the body of the second fly, extinguishing its already-waning life. He opened the fist of his right hand and dropped the tiny corpse into his hand with the first, then popped both carcasses into his mouth together. He bit down and there was a tiny, albeit satisfying, crunch. He chewed for a moment and sucked the poor creatures back into his throat.

Leaning back against the pitiful excuse for a bed, Renfield turned his head to look through the crack in the wall. Outside, the Transylvanian skyline bled a vibrant yellow, the woods and roads ablaze with it. The tiny point of the castle was a knife piercing the belly of the clouds above. He remembered briefly the awful, howling scream he had heard during the night, coming not from inside the madhouse as usual but from the direction of the castle. He was almost convinced he must have dreamt it.

Almost.

The bars of his cell shrieked open and he wheeled around, yanked from his reverie by the squeal of the poorly-oiled hinges. With wide eyes he looked up at the looming figure who'd stepped into the room, a hulking mountain of a man who looked as though he'd been carved from the same granite the madhouse was made from. The warden was a bulk of thick, scarred flesh and thatched hair, dressed in a sweaty cloth vest and a long, dark overcoat. Thick knots of stone-grey hair hung down to his shoulders and his face was a hard, stubbled brick. A tall, stiff knot of leather poked out from his belt, the looping coils of a tarred whip slung through each other in a sick, black spiral.

"Up, Insect Boy," the warden said, his voice heavy and thick with the sharp points of his Moldavian accent. "On feet now."

Carefully Renfield stood, his legs and body weak with a lack of nutrition; were he allowed a looking glass, he might have seen that his skin was as pale as death, that his eyes were sunk into the pits of his sockets and his cheeks sallow and thin. Still young physically, and still relatively fit despite his treatment, a proper look at him would tell anybody that this was the spirit of an old man in a young man's body. That he had already died a thousand deaths.

"Fool has not eaten," the warden said flatly, gesturing to the bowl on the floor.

"It served its purpose," Renfield said of the food.

The warden shrugged, enormous shoulders bulging with thick clumps of tendon. "Will serve purpose again this morning," he said simply. "No breakfast for man who refuse dinner."

"Fine," Renfield said calmly.

More flies would come to a steadily-rotting meal from the night before than to a fresh pot of gruel, more vessels of lifeblood for him to absorb, and he knew that there was far more nutrition in the bodies of the living creatures that came in from outside than in the slop he was served here; the warden wouldn't understand, but Renfield would not have expected this mass of meat and violence to understand much of anything.

The hulking shadow took a step closer. "You are talking back to me, no?"

"No," Renfield said, as firmly as possible.

"You are," the warden whispered, leaning close enough that Renfield could smell paprika on his breath. "Little bug boy is talking back to me."

Renfield said nothing. Images crashed inevitably into his mind, unstoppable: his mother towering above him, his father's belt in her hand; the drunken wretch of a woman striking her cowering child across the face with a bony hand; the smell of ale on her breath and tar on her fingers as she jammed them into the soft, fleshy pits around his eyes until dark shapes swelled in his vision.

A thin, black smile split the warden's face and his eyes flashed with bloodlust. "You are insolent little boy," he hissed. "Punishment for you."

Renfield heard the *crack* of the whip before he saw the warden reach for his belt. Warmth spread across his face even before he registered the stinging pain that lashed his cheek, and he stumbled back onto the bed, sinking onto his rump as the enormous man laughed. The whip snaked back into the dark and he raised his hands in front of his face. "Please," he moaned, "I didn't mean—"

The leathery tail of the whip shot out again and struck his wrists. He yowled and shrunk back into the corner of the cell, his arms trembling as bolts of agony shot into his hands. The third *crack* of the whip echoed through his entire body as the tail ripped into his side, where undoubtedly a great red welt would form across his ribs in a few hours' time and join the others. For now, all that existed there was pain.

It was minutes later that he realised the warden had left his cell and that he was alone again.

Renfield sobbed quietly for a while, the relentless screaming of the madhouse ringing in his ears. He felt a buzzing in his stomach and crawled out of bed, his entire body aching bitterly as he slunk across the cell and relieved himself in the metal pail by the bars. There came a leering whoop from across the corridor as he exposed himself. He barely heard it.

Eventually he returned to the wall, planting his rump on the stone floor and looking out through the tiny crack between the bricks. The paltry view was sparse and unsympathetic; the mountains stared coldly back at him, their pale crests painted with a pinkish sunlight so that they appeared to have been slathered with milk and blood. Somewhere in the woods, a wild dog howled.

Renfield pressed his cheek to the wall and absent-mindedly poked his hand into the crack, rubbing harsh brick dust into the pads of his fingers. There was a soft fluttering as stony particles drifted into the cell, briefly carrying the sunlight with them before darkening in the air and gently spraying the floor.

The brick wobbled a little beneath his fingers, like a sore tooth that is nearly ready to be plucked from the gum.

Renfield froze. After a moment, he gently pressed at the stone again. His bony fingers were not strong enough to pry the thing free, but there was some give.

Cautiously, he reached down and withdrew the spoon from his putrid wooden bowl.

Gently Renfield slid it into the crack and pushed upward, using the spoon like a tiny fulcrum. For a while, there was nothing, and after a few minutes the spoon bent in surrender. Grunting impatiently, the boy pulled the spoon free and straightened it again, thrusting it desperately back into the tiny hole.

A tiny spout of brick dust jetted from the wall as a crack opened beneath the loose stone. He almost whooped with triumph, then remembered himself. Glancing back into the corridor to ensure he was not being watched, Renfield clamped the spoon beneath his teeth and returned his attention to the crack. With some effort he dug his hand inside and bent his fingers inward.

Like blood from a sore, the stone popped out of its nook in the wall and fell with a dull *thok* onto the floor. For a moment Renfield stared at the thing, the tiny lump of stone that had landed at his feet, and then he looked out through the gaping hole in the wall and grinned.

Clutching the stone in his narrow fingers, the boy pressed his eye to the ragged hole and gazed out upon the gravelly labyrinth of Transylvanian roads that extended from the madhouse. With his free hand, he reached gravely through the hole and flexed his fingers in the sunlight.

Gripping the stone a little tighter in his hand, Renfield licked his lips and smiled.

Mother was asleep at the kitchen table, her head lolled forward on angular shoulders, her nightgown spattered with blood-red drops of wine. In her left hand, she tightly gripped a serrated steak knife, and on the table before her was a shredded journal of yellowed paper and scrawled, spidery handwriting; she had attacked the thing quite viciously with the knife, ripping hunks from the pages and utterly destroying the leather spine.

Now she snored delicately, the knife hovering in a trembling fist as though set to strike again, when really her elbow was propped quite naturally on the edge of the table. A half-drunk bottle of *Grasă de Cotnari* stood nearby, the glass scored in places where she had half-heartedly scraped it with the knife. The awful shriek had woken Renfield; the sobbing that had come after had kept him that way.

Now the child stood in the doorway of the kitchen, watching the spindly woman's back heave as she drew in sharp, ragged breaths. The journal was his father's, a diary of sorts which he had used, it seemed, as some sort of therapeutic release, detailing his inner thoughts right until the day he'd left them. Presumably he had bought a new journal then, having forgotten to take this one with him. Or maybe he had left it deliberately for her to find, knowing that it would upset her.

Renfield didn't really see the use of diaries.

The body in the chair bobbed its head, perhaps unsettled by some aspect of the dream it was dreaming, and Renfield stepped into the kitchen, his bare feet padding quietly on the cold tiles. He approached his mother with some unease, his eyes fixed on the knife.

The boy paused, blinking. He could smell rotting *impletata*, could hear people screaming somewhere. But the smell was in his peripheral and its direction unidentifiable; the agonised howls all around were muffled enough that he fancied he must be imagining them.

He stood beside his mother and tightened his tiny

fingers around the ornamental clock he'd retrieved from the cabinet in her bedroom. He trembled uncontrollably, standing close enough to her that, were she to awaken at any moment, she would strike him. Her grip on the knife was fluid, her knuckles contracting and opening every few seconds, flexing in response to her actions in the dreamworld. She had cut Renfield with this very knife, more than once. But it was her hands that he feared: the furious smack of her palm against his cheek, the dreadful tightening of her stained fingers around his neck.

Well, enough was enough.

Somewhere in the very back of his skull he heard another sound: a scream unlike the others, the scream of badly-oiled hinges peeling open. He felt the shadows of a row of iron bars falling across his body and, just for a moment, he felt the cold stone floor pressed to the pads of his feet. Another shadow consumed him, the shadow of a mountainous, greasy-haired monster, and he grew cold; and there, a breeze, drifting in through a small hole in the wall of the cell and brushing his ankle like delicate fingers…

But then the sensation was gone, and all the child knew was that he had to act.

Renfield moved quickly, placing himself directly behind his sleeping mother and raising his little fist high. The clock was heavy, a beautiful and ornate brick of swirling French brass and ivory facing. It was still ticking as he held it above her head, his little body frozen momentarily in the act. Ticking too fast, almost anxiously: *Tok-tok-tok-tok-tok—*

The sleeping woman's eyes snapped open, and she tipped her head up and back to look at him, her neck bending at an unnatural angle. She grinned, teeth flashing in a cruel, drunken face. "What you doing with that, insolent boy?" she spat, and her voice was all wrong: it was a man's voice, thick with an accent that wasn't hers and gravelly from years of yelling and shouting.

"You won't hurt me anymore," the young Renfield whispered, and he brought the clock down in a violent arc of gold plating.

The flat base of the clock sunk into her temple with an awful, sick *crack* and her eyes bulged. The steak knife tumbled from her hand and clattered onto the stone beneath them and Renfield's gaze flickered to it: not a knife, in fact, but a coiled, tar-stroked whip, the fall smeared with fresh blood. His mother gasped, her whole body rocking back in the chair, and his attention snapped back to her. There was a terrible dent in her forehead, as though her skull were made of some kind of flesh-coloured putty. Somewhere there was shrieking laughter; through the crack in the wall, a buzzing fly entered and, oblivious to the situation, landed hungrily on the rotting forcemeat in the bowl.

"Put that... down..." the warden rasped with the

drunken woman's mouth. Her head still tipped back, she raised a trembling hand to her forehead to press the pads of her fingers to the growing red welt there. Renfield noticed now that one of her eyes had clouded with red. He smiled.

"No," he whispered, and he brought it crashing down again. The corner of the heavy clock smashed into her brow, catching two of her fingertips too, and he heard bone snap. The force was enough to tip her back on her chair and she crashed to the kitchen floor and then he was upon her, gripping the clock with both hands and smashing it into her face.

"You won't hurt me again!" he shrieked, ignoring the wet *splotch* of bone sinking into muscle and dragging the clock up once more. He pounded it into her mouth and felt the *crunch* of bone reverberate through his entire body as her jaw shattered. "Never again!"

With one final blow of his whole body he slammed the clock into her nose and followed through with all his strength. Her face caved in and the gasping stopped as a sliver of bone slipped into her brain stem. The boy withdrew, panting, exhilarated.

He dropped the stone to the floor and a small cloud of dust exploded around it.

The warden lay dead at Renfield's feet, twitching gently. A mountain of meat and muscle in stinking linen, his skull broken inward and bloody.

"You'll never hurt me again, you dog," Renfield whispered, his chest heaving. His eyes darted to the keys hanging from the warden's belt, then up to the open iron bars. All around him, the very walls of the madhouse howled. "That goes for both of you."

He knew the outside was real because the smell was unbearable; rather than the sweet, pleasant scent of flowers he was greeted by a thick haze of horse manure and stale petrichor. The young man staggered dumbly onto the road, his legs weak and unused to carrying his weight. Pivoting drunkenly to look back, Renfield gazed up at the asylum and grinned. The building loomed over him like some gargantuan tombstone, crashing out of the mist and grinning with a million tiny barred mouths, iron teeth glinting in the softly bleeding sunlight. Inside, the wailing and shrieking and agonised yelps of the inmates were muffled through layers of brick and stone and madness.

He was free.

Renfield wheeled his body away from the madhouse and stumbled uphill, the cracked earth of the road a sharp, gritty blessing on his bare feet. Everything out here was dry and cool and when he swayed onto the edges of the path the grass scratched at the flesh of his ankles. The slopes of the mountains – impossibly close now, despite his being only a few dozen yards nearer to them – swelled and waned all around the edges of his vision, sharp peaks thrusting messily into the clouds where they were split and bent by soft, grey shapes.

Between here and the mountains were the forests, and the rolling hills upon which the pines were rooted, and somewhere out there was the tall, straight spire of the castle, though it seemed to have disappeared for now into the fog.

He began to laugh, and soon his quiet triumph exploded from his belly in a thick, throaty cackle. His tongue and mouth hurt and his knees were weak; he needed to sit, or to lay down, but he would distance himself a little more from the asylum first. He was free, finally free, and he would not return to the madhouse, nor any other, for as long as he was alive.

He had not let go of the stone. A smear of blood and matted hair painted its sharp edge red. The slight scent of pennies was almost enough to drive him truly mad.

After walking for a little over a mile, he saw a smudge of black on the road ahead and slowed himself. It would be a terrible thing to meet one of the wardens between here and their home in the village; warily he pressed forward, keeping his eyes on the shape. It did not seem to be moving.

As he drew nearer Renfield saw that it was a carriage, the tall black horse pulling it standing impatiently on the path. It scuffed at the earth with its hooves as he approached, but stayed obediently put.

The carriage was dark and plain, undecorated. A quick glance inside told him that it was empty. The owner must have gotten out to stretch their legs – or else been snatched by one of the wild animals of the forest. Stranger things had happened. Renfield's eyes darted about wickedly as he moved slowly around the carriage. Perhaps this was his chance; perhaps he could escape—

Bzzz.

He froze at the sound, his pale face twisted in recognition. His stomach growled hungrily and his hand moved slowly to his gut, where the skin was bruised and overly malleable beneath his shirt. Wary of the horse's hind quarters, he stepped closer to the great dark-haired animal and caught sight of the insect buzzing about its muscular flank. As it landed on the beast's thigh a great sash of tail hair whipped angrily at it; the fly continued unperturbed.

Bzzzzz.

"Delicious," Renfield whispered, taking another cautious step and outstretching his hand. "Oh, delicious life…"

"Hullo there, old chap!" came a loud voice from behind him, and Renfield's head snapped around to look.

A youngish gentleman in the smart – yet affordable – garments of a student approached from the trees beyond the road, fixing his belt with both hands as he stumbled toward the carriage. His suit was a sharp palette of grey, and his hair was thick and black and combed neatly across a straight, flat brow. His eyes sparkled with youth and passion. He paused at the sight of Renfield, then grinned at the strange man as though greeting a friend.

"You know how it is on these long journeys," the young man said, coming up to the horse and offering Renfield his hand. "One has to relieve oneself upward of a dozen times, especially on these colder days."

"Your carriage," Renfield said, only now hearing himself speak for the first time in years without the abhorrent backdrop of screams which had accompanied his voice for so long.

"Why, yes," said the young man. He looked Renfield up and down, as though seeing him for the first time. Behind them, the fly had settled into the horse's dark fur and was quite cheerily ignoring the thick tail that beat regularly at it.

"Say, you look like you need a ride. Into the village, perhaps?"

Renfield smiled thinly. "Would be... much appreciated," he said carefully.

"Jolly good. I'm heading for the school, so that's on my way. Studying medicine, don't you know?" The young man grinned. "One of these days, I hope to find work treating those ill of the mind. You know the

44

type?"

Renfield smiled ruefully.

"Well then," the student nodded briskly, "come on with you. We should do well not to stand about out here all day – I've heard there are most awful creatures in these parts."

He stepped swiftly to the cab and swung open the door, gesturing for Renfield to follow. As he stepped up onto the carriage, he turned back and asked: "Say, what's your name, fellow?"

"Renfield," the scrawny creature replied after a beat. "And yours?"

"Seward," the young man smiled. "John Seward. Now, let's get out of these woods and back to sanity, shall we?"

MOONLIT VALLEY, TASTE OF BLOOD

(Moonlight.)

The long, clawed shadows of aspen and birch trees stretched languidly downhill, extending from the knotted feet of the forest's edge and snaking between scattered chunks of earth. Sharp tufts of grass glowed a pale grey-blue, ruffled by a wind that whistled softly out of the woods.

This shrill whisper of warning was lost by the time it reached the base of the slope, where the flickering amber light of a campfire fought desperately against the darkening of the hillock. It was losing.

Darkness gathered between the trees on the hilltop, swelling and flooding every empty space so that the woods seemed thicker and more cloying than they might in the daylight. Strings of shadow crept up through ragged rivets in each trunk, slipping between cracks in the wood so that it looked like the trees were weeping, thick black tears drizzling downward from upper branches in which decrepit, abandoned birds' nests hung like the husks of decaying prehistoric insects. The branches themselves were still full and flushed with the last touches of summer, but a bitter cold rifled them.

The shape lumbered heavily through the pitch-dark of the forest, her movements shambling and slow. She was enormous, but her padded feet made no sound as they pressed into the earth. Despite her size, leathery skin covered with dark, matted fur made her almost invisible in the shadows, but the moonlight was reflected in her eyes: two flaring points of green burned hungrily in the sleek, canid silhouette of her skull as she moved.

(Water babbling somewhere close by, trickling gently over sharp stone ridges.)

The shadows around her parted as she reached the edge of the forest and glared down toward the foot of the hill. Thick bunches of muscle in her neck and shoulders rippled as plumes of breath erupted from wet, shining nostrils; black lips peeled back and gluey strings of saliva dribbled down a scarred chin. Fresh, deep wounds across her throat and the top of her head were sprinkled with wet flecks of blood, not yet fully healed. Her chest and ribs were punctured and scraped, new cuts ripping through patches of old scar tissue. In places her fur was so thick with blood that it formed thick, tangled knots down her back, ribbons of sticky red running through the sharp bumps of her spine.

(Stars filtered out by thick banks of black cloud. Ink

staining the horizon.)

Even in the limited light, she could make out every detail of the campsite below.

The slope upon which she stood keened down into a valley that tumbled haphazardly into the wasteland beyond, a carpet of half-dead grass laid over a hard, bumpy surface. Patches of dry earth were so barren and cracked that nothing grew, and in the cracks only absolute blackness prevailed. Where there was life, it was sparse: the insects skittering through the undergrowth were tiny and irrelevant; the flowers were spiked and colourless. This land, and the land beyond, was her territory, her home. The flowers knew not to grow here. Behind her and beneath the hills, the planes were vast and filled with prey – an adequate hunting ground for the creature and her brothers.

Tonight, the hunting ground was splayed before her in a mass of firelit canvas.

A thin smile spread across her snout, sharp, serrated teeth flashing wet and white as a low growl rumbled deep in her belly. Those teeth were chipped and cracked, some stained orange with blood, others smashed upward and into each other so that they protruded at hellish angles from split gums. Her maw was a ruin of bone, her jawbone crooked to one side. The moonlight didn't reach her here, and the lenses of her eyes no longer reflected it as a pair of bright, glaring discs; rather, the firelight from below caught on tufts of her fur and painted them a greasy yellow, and her eyes were black balls of glass, one slightly narrower than the other between pressed, blood-encrusted lids.

(The rattle of faraway cicadas.)

The campsite was small, spread across a section of the valley that was relatively flat. Six or seven canvas tents had been erected in a circle around a campfire that glistened wetly, tongues of orange lapping at half-chewed chunks of wood and roughly-sawn logs. Nearer the fire, a selection of crude seats had been arranged into another, smaller ring, seats made of empty barrels and mossy lumps of rock. Between the tents, temporary structures stood beneath thin fabric shelters. A hastily-constructed wooden rack served as a log store beside one of the larger tents; elsewhere, a neat stack of gasoline canisters had spilled into an arrangement of large water canteens. A battered Jeep had been parked between two identical, mid-sized green tents.

Beside the largest of the tents, a large, rectangular shape was obscured by a thick woollen blanket. Tar-stained ropes had been strapped across the top of the boxlike thing, tied around the heads of thick, iron posts slammed into the ground.

The creature stood on her hind legs, chest heaving as hungry breaths wracked her ribs. Her body lilted as she dug her claws into the trunk of an aspen beside her, shifting her weight into an arm run through with thick, stringy muscles. The snarl of her maw became a furious, gritted mess of pointed teeth as she bowed her head and prepared to strike. Shoulders back, rippling, her body hunched as though ready to pounce. The hand gripping the tree flexed and twisted, rows of knuckles popping as they rolled over each other, claws grinding and pulling at the bark. A sinewy paw rose to her snout and she wiped away thick gobs of saliva, ripping them from her mouth like she was tearing the skin of her maw away, flinging spittle into the trees.

Many of the campers had left the fire for the shelter of their tents, and now the last of them began to move. A male and a female, bundled in dark cloths. The woman's throat was gripped by the frayed fingers of a blood-red scarf, her yellow hair tossed by the wind. He stood first, then offered his hand to her. Ignoring it, she stood awkwardly and stretched. His arm fell and the creature watched his face change. There was a bitterness there, illuminated by the firelight, that his mate had not noticed. Tension rippled in the darkness between the two.

The woman finished stretching and turned to her partner, kissing him briefly. The face he made in response conveyed satisfaction; when the woman turned her back and began to walk toward the nearest tent, the creature noted, his expression changed again. He followed her to the shelter, passing beneath a fluorescent tether and ducking into the tent with her. The firelight followed them inside and for a moment their silhouettes were dashed onto the thin, canvas walls. The creature watched through a plume of warm breath as the two figures melted into each other in the small space, becoming indiscernible as the skin of the tent rippled, and as the first shadow leant back to zip the door closed, the firelight was cast out and the tent went dark.

The creature's movement was like a flood of black water gushing out of a ruptured cell: her body slumped forward as she planted four paws firmly in the earth. A metric tonne of meat and power bristled, back arched, eyes flaring once again as the moonlight pricked at them. Her breathing had become calm and natural, her heels bent like springs. Gently, she padded down the hill. Stepping slowly at first, easing her claws into the grass and digging her heels back; gravity carried her through the shadows and allowed her to lope forward with minimal effort.

Halfway down the slope
(Crackling embers, smell of smoke.)
she launched herself into a sprint.

She was a wraith of moonlit fur and thick, powerful tissue. Her hind legs were like trunks, her claws slamming into the earth as her calves took the brunt of the impact, thick tendons snapping taut as they extended in mid-air. The glow of the moon dashed her eyes like fire and her teeth ground together, thick gobs of saliva ripping back from her snout as the wind exploded past her.

The beast careened into the campsite with such force that thin, firelit clouds of dust were thrown up from the ground behind her. She splayed her claws and her whole body so that she was instantly still; she sniffed, though the smell of meat all around her was strong enough that she could tell which of the campers had bathed least recently. Her smooth, wet nose twitched, pointed ears pinned back against her skull like the leathery wings of a bat. She listened.

A dozen gently throbbing heartbeats were spread through the camp around her, each one sending gentle ribbons of vibration across the molecules in the air. Most were slowed, their owners unconscious. Over the soft crackling of the dying fire, she heard twelve lives pulsing steadily, twelve pumping stems of lifeblood protected only by thin flesh and thinner canvas sheets.

(Another heartbeat, duller and slower than the rest, though its owner did not sleep.)

She turned her head toward the nearest pulse, eyes falling upon a stained, green tent. It had been lazily erected and sagged in the middle; its single inhabitant was snoring loudly. One of the older men. The creature's lips peeled back and she grinned.

She sprang into the air like a panther and pounced, ploughing the full weight of her body into her forearms and burying them deep in the canvas folds of the tent. Immediately she rolled forward, ripping the tent from its flimsy tethers and almost folding it in half. There was a faint cry from somewhere inside the mess of canvas and fur but it was smothered, useless – crashing into the ground, the beast raised a single paw and extended her claws before smashing them exactly and deliberately into the middle of the bundle of rope and fabric she'd gathered beneath her. Bony knuckles popped as her paw flexed, a foot long and decorated with straining sinews. Blood spurted inside the tent and thin strings of viscera erupted through the ragged holes in the canvas. She felt hot meat twitching around her claws and twisted; a tight, dreadful gasp from inside the tent, and then silence. She lay atop the broken frame of the tent for a moment, waiting until the carcass inside had stopped convulsing, and then with a soft sucking sound she withdrew her claws and stood.

On her hind legs, she was a giant.

Ichor stained her claws and dripped slowly into the grass. She was a gargantuan thing, looming over the campsite even though her shoulders were hunched, her drooling snout dipped low. Her thick, tangled fur would have been streaked with copper and grey in the daylight, but in the dark she was as black as the shadows. She stood on long, slender calves that crashed into angular knees and powerful thighs, bones popping and cracking as she breathed heavily and the entire weight of her body shifted and moved on her ankles. Her claws were gnarled hooks of bone, inches long and granite-grey. At the ends of her arms, longer, thinner claws exploded from fingers that were almost human. But her hands were like hammers, the bones stretched and hideous, and the knuckles were a mess of chunks beneath thin, leathery flesh stretched tight.

Her eyes were wet with mourning. A sheen of rage bristled across glassy lenses; beneath, they shimmered with sorrow.

Falling onto her paws again, she padded toward the next tent and circled. She had mastered the practice of stalking her prey, and the slaughter of the first man had been carried out with barely a sound despite her enormous size and weight. Thick bunches of fur rippled across her shoulders and back as she moved silently around the tent. Her skull was massive and heavy but the muscles of her neck were thick enough to carry it deftly; her features were doglike and cruel, but her body was more human than hound; all at once bulky and sleek, huge and angry but spirit-like and delicate.

There were three in this tent. Female, all of them, pressed in tight together. Wrapped in thick blankets and cassocks so that their heartbeats were muffled.

She smiled.

Pressing her snout forward, the creature raised a paw and carefully – almost gingerly – pressed the very points of her claws to the canvas. The coppery tang of blood lilted on the smoky air now, clouding her senses; as this went on, and as more blood flowed into the earth, it would become more and more difficult to remain focused. But in this moment, her motivations were razor-sharp.

She swiped. Her claws knifed through the canvas like blades through milk and she plunged a fist inside, knuckles cracking outward as she reached for the nearest of the women. One of the three pulses nearest to her quickened suddenly as one of the women started to wake. Fast; this had to be fast—

The beast smashed her claws downward, rolling her shoulder into the strike. There was a sick, dry crack as the women's ribs caved in and a wet splurt of blood. The brief wriggle of a punctured lung. She squeezed, claws piercing muscle easily. The sleeping woman moaned; something popped wetly in the creature's fist. She sensed movement – one of the other women clumsily propping herself up onto her elbows – and in a blur of blood-soaked fur withdrew her claws and thrust her arm across the tent. An enormous paw clamped over the second woman's face before she could scream. Thick, padded leather filled her mouth and the creature squeezed. The woman twitched, one arm tangled in a thick fold of blankets, the other coming up to bat madly at the creature's wrist.

Her claws slid into the woman's skull with little more than a whisper and she thrust the heel of her paw backward, ramming it into the poor thing's chin and snapping her neck with a loud crunch.

The woman's body fell limp. Snuffling, lips peeled back and eyes bright with hunger, the beast pushed her head into the tent and sniffed deeply. Something moved in the cramped shadows of the broken shelter, scuffling away from her. The third woman was awake, alert, her heartbeat desperate and pounding; she scrambled back against the wall of the tent but there was nowhere to go.

The creature turned her head and grinned, lapping her smashed teeth with a thick, grey tongue. A naked, dark-skinned woman clutched at her friend's neck, the dead thing's head lolling uselessly in her lap. She breathed heavily, desperately scrambling with bloody fingers, searching for a pulse despite the gory hole in her sister's chest. Her head shot up, a mess of black hair falling in her face; her eyes snapped open wide as she saw the creature's teeth.

The beast felt it coming: a scream building in the woman's throat, rising like bile. She did nothing to stop it. There was a delicious kind of satisfaction in the achievement of a stealthy kill, but it was time now for a little… noise.

After all, didn't these men deserve to die

screaming?

The naked woman shrieked, her throat exploding with a yell of fear ripping so violently at her vocal cords that it began to fluctuate within a few seconds. Her chest heaved as the agonised yell fell dead in her mouth. It built back up in her chest, and now the beast could hear the murmurs and hazy whisperings of men waking all around the camp; the woman screamed again, and those murmurs became calls and shouts.

The creature smiled.

The screaming stopped suddenly. Realisation flooded the woman's eyes, and she opened her mouth again, lips quivering, entire body shivering with fear – not to scream for a third time, but to speak—

Then the beast opened her jaws wide and thrust her neck into the tent, clamping her serrated teeth down on the woman's throat and gorging herself hungrily on chunks of cartilage and spine, and the delicate thing's words were lost to the wet, snuffling sounds of meat and blood slipping down the creature's throat.

The campsite exploded with noise, the shredding of tents opening shattered by the yells and cries of the bleary men pouring from them. The creature stepped back, great head swinging left and right as she took it all in.

"Over there!" yelled a gruff-looking, middle-aged

man with an impressive mount of facial hair on his upper lip. The creature swung her snout in his direction and growled, instantly recognising the scratched barrel of the hunting rifle crooked under his arm. He was dressed in grass-stained khakis and boots; most of the campers seemed to have gone to bed fully clothed. The other side of the campfire, a male and female in brown furs and scarves were crawling from a low, white mess of a tent pitched beside a wooden rack of spears and what looked like a half-barrel filled with kitchen utensils.

Footsteps behind her.

The beast pivoted her upper body and swung, pitching her claws into the stalker's chest. The man's eyes bulged; he was large, his belly straining out of a blood-spattered cook's uniform, his hair grey and greasy. As the creature twisted her claws into the meat between his ribs, his grip on a large, heavy rolling pin loosened and it tumbled to the ground between his feet. The man's cheeks reddened as she yanked her fist out of him and thrust a knee up into his groin. A grunt escaped him and he wobbled backward; she turned, alert to the presence of another figure in her peripheral.

"Eat shit, mangy dog!" screamed a tall, square-shouldered woman with frizzy bed-hair and a Flintlock. She glared up into the beast's eyes and squeezed the trigger.

An explosion of sound rocked from the barrel of the

battered gun and shot sprayed the air between them. Already the creature was on all fours – a carnage of tiny pellets splashed her back and warmth spread between her enormous shoulder blades – and she launched herself into the woman's midriff, knocking her to the ground. The gun fell uselessly away and the beast opened her maw wide, punching both clawed fists into the attacker's sides and bellowing. Her roar was deep and long and might have sounded like thunder to anyone nearby; tinged with spittle, hot breath blossomed in the square-shouldered woman's face and she screeched.

(Across the campfire, the click of a safety catch.)

The beast reeled back before the hunting rifle could fire, turning on her heels and lurching into the shadows at the edge of the campsite. A thick bang echoed through the valley and the smell of gunpowder fused with blood in the air. The cook scrambled for his rolling pin in the ground, knees scuffing the grass as a wall of slick, shining red flowed down his belly from the wounds in his chest.

"Where's it gone?" yelled the man with the grey moustache, popping another shell into his hunting rifle. The other side of the fire, two younger women grabbed a spear each from the rack and whirled around, brandishing them into the dark.

Silence. No sound for a single, pregnant beat except the crackling of the flames and the fractured moans of the square-shouldered woman. The beast had disappeared.

Padding footsteps near the Jeep. Scraping claws.

"There!" a bald, Black man yelled, still half-bundled in the folds of his tent. He thrust an arm out of the opening, the steel of a loaded pistol glistening in his hand. He swung it in the direction of the sound—

Nothing there. The shadows around the Jeep were still and lifeless.

"Bastard thing!" scoffed the man with the hunting rifle. Around him, more men were stumbling from their tents and pulling weapons from their clothes. "There's more of us than even you can handle, beast!"

A thick flutter. Panicked, one woman punched both arms into the air and shot upwards with a crack and an explosion of gunsmoke. The shriek of a tawny owl trilled across the valley as the bird darted off-course. Somewhere, an empty cartridge tinkled over a spray of gravel in the grass.

A second. Two.

Nothing.

"Maybe it's gone," one of the campers whispered. Another nodded in agreement.

"We should pack up," a woman in linen pyjamas said. "Move on before it comes back."

"It ain't coming back," the cook growled, heaving himself to his feet and slamming the rolling pin into his palm. "Not if I've got anything to do with—"

A shadow with flaring green eyes erupted from his back like a pair of huge, clawed wings and immediately seemed to fold around him. His head was enveloped as the beast slammed her jaws around his skull and ripped upwards. Ribbons of blood sprayed a nearby tent as the flesh of his throat stretched, snapped and tore open.

He stood for a moment, gushing lifeblood from the red raw stump of his neck, then slowly, clumsily, he toppled forward. His head fell into the grass somewhere behind him and rolled, wide-eyed.

Somebody screamed.

The creature stood in the burly cook's place, a mountain of sinew and fur that heaved with thick, hungry breaths in the dark. Her ears were pointed and alert, twitching with the movements of every particle of air and dust. Embers scattered in manic clouds from the fire, now fanned by oxygen and alive again, sprinkling her body with tiny sparks of amber. Claws spread into great webs of bone on either side of her, head cocked to one side, she stared across the fire as the barrels of half a dozen weapons were swung in her direction.

She caught the eye of the man with the hunting rifle. His face was set in a stoic, grim mask of acceptance; he understood why she'd come, why she'd targeted them, but it was too late now. They couldn't fix that.

Only she could fix it.

A single bead of sweat ran down his brow, furrowed into a tight frown. His irises shone with the deep, smouldering red of the campfire. He pointed the rifle at her and spoke quietly, his voice almost a whisper. The fibres of his moustache twitched as his mouth moved carefully, deliberately. An ember fell onto his breast and burned a tiny, black hole into his overcoat.

"Go," he said, "and there will be no trouble."

A moment of hesitation: he was wondering if she could understand their language. If perhaps she had once been of their species, of their cruel ilk; if something had turned her. He was wondering if there was still anything left, somewhere within the canid abomination standing before him, of who she had once been.

She smiled thinly, serrated teeth glistening with sinew and blood. And remained exactly where she stood.

It was enough.

The hunter brought up the rifle soundlessly, raising the sight from the creature's chest to her snout with one fluid movement and squeezing the trigger. There was no visible recoil; the butt of the rifle was perfectly contained in the meat of his shoulder. The barrel exploded.

The point of the bullet smacked her between the eyes and the casing shattered, tiny slivers of lead unfurling from the broken thing as a useless chunk bounced away and fell silently into the grass. The crack of the rifle was still echoing.

The creature didn't move, didn't flinch. The bullet had scorched her fur and left a blackened patch the size of a penny smouldering above her right eye, but it hadn't broken the skin. The man with the hunting rifle opened his mouth in shock, lowering the thing. Another scream from across the camp, and a moment of utter despair…

The beast flexed her knuckles, tilting her head from one side to the next and loudly cracking the muscles in her neck. Her shoulders rolled forward, thick, black spines of fur shivering across her back.

Her head tipped up into the moonlight, and she howled.

The valley erupted with sound, dreadful banks of canid noise rippling into the hills. A murmuration of tiny birds exploded from the nearest aspen and scattered. It was a banshee's maddening shriek, pitched down with a great fiery bellow from somewhere within the beast's gut, a swelling roar of pain and anger and heartbreak that flooded the air and choked the very heart of the campfire so that the flames, just for a moment, sunk back into themselves and turned a sickly black.

The man with the impressive moustache and the hunting rifle looked up. His comrades followed, half a dozen pairs of eyes turning to the top of the hill above them. To the crown of woodland at its peak, a strip of crooked trunks and shadows that rolled across the slope and shivered in the wind.

The trees were moving.

"Oh, good lord..."

The shadows stretched and bent and split in two, welling around the bases of the trees and spreading downhill. Shapes in the black – shapes that were the black – became more real with every step. Ten of them, fifteen – thirty – thirty gargantuan shapes coming forth from the dark of the forest and crawling on all fours downhill. A few of the pack lurched into a sprint halfway to the campsite, others spreading around the valley, slipping into banks of shadow in the hills, surrounding them... horribly deformed monsters, shapeless in the dark but hideously, undeniably wolflike.

She stalked forward slowly, moving on all fours, slinking through the dark like a ghost. Around her, the creature's brothers burst out from the craggy walls of the valley and screamed into the campsite, tearing through canvas and meat as they snatched screaming bundles of lifeblood into the dark. Carnage.

The man with the hunting rifle didn't move. Couldn't. His eyes were wide and shining with terror, his lip quivering. He stared at her as she prowled steadily toward him, the firelight between them curling in on itself, chunks of wood igniting as it began to spread, unburdened and encouraged by the chaos around them. Dry grass caught and shot into yellow flame; thick gobs of spittle oozed from cracks in the wood and hissed as they dripped into the ash below.

She stood as she reached the campfire, rising again to her full height. Still a good eight or ten feet from where the man stood, she towered above him. She was a monument, a great clawed obelisk of vengeance, and he was nothing at all. Around them, the screaming grew quieter; the snarls and bellows of the pack were the dominant beats of a grisly soundtrack, music to accompany the great shifting mass of streaked black fur and flopping red flesh around them that swirled and bent like a whirlwind.

"I'm sorry," he whispered weakly, but it was too late.

Her throat opened in a savage roar and she ploughed through the fire, thick flames of amber surging around her. Her chest and shoulders were scattered with embers, a great glowing blanket of them enveloping her back. Her eyes blazed orange as she lunged, punching her claws into his chest and throwing him to the ground. They tumbled together, a mountain of flaming fur and her prey, her growling maw less than an inch from his face, her eyes burning furiously into his. His back smacked the earth and something snapped loudly.

"Please," he whimpered, "please, please…"

The creature turned him over easily, slamming a paw into his broken back and pressing his chest into the dirt. Behind them, her brothers had finished; trails of blood and hair lay between burnt and burning patches of grass, and the beasts sat slavering at the edges of the campsite, dozens of flecks of moonlight burning in blood-soaked faces.

She dug claws into the man's hair and yanked up his head. Made him look at it.

"I'm sorry," he moaned, "please…"

She dropped him with a satisfied growl. He sobbed into the bloody grass, twitching as ribbons of pain shot through his back. Slowly, she moved past him and padded between the two largest tents. For a moment she just listened.

Before her, whispers of shadow trawled the back of a squarish container, a crate covered with blankets and rope. Inside, that heartbeat: slow, weak. Beaten.

Carefully, she slid a bony claw forward and severed one of the thick, frayed ropes pinned to the ground. It shot upward and slipped back across the top of the thing. The stained blanket that covered it billowed in the breeze. The creature reached for it with a thick, bony paw that was almost delicate, ripped it away and cast it to the ground. The corner of the blanket set alight almost instantly; behind her, one of the tents was ablaze. Her face burned with streaks of orange.

As the thing beneath the blanket was revealed, her brothers began to howl. A chorus of sorrow that echoed up into the hills and melded with the moonlight.

The cage must have been four feet high and four wide, the thick iron bars black and straight. The steel floor of the thing had been lined with horsehair and straw and it stunk of urine and blood. Thick, purple-splashed tangles of wolfsbane hung from the top of the cage and twisted through the bars. A fat iron padlock hung from the horizontal bars across the door.

The pup lay panting in a crude nest of straw, her malnourished frame no larger than that of a human child. Her snout and nose were dry and her fur was covered in patches of dried blood. The creature's heart flooded suddenly with emotion, with heartbreak and relief and hatred and passion all at once. In the earth behind her the man with the moustache scrambled desperately for the hunting rifle he'd dropped. She ignored him.

The poor thing in the cage opened one bruised eye as wide as it could, the lids almost fused together. The infant was still pink and fresh, her skin wrinkled where it was exposed between ragged spots of wispy fur. Tracks of deep red crisscrossed her rump and hind.

Rage exploded in the beast's heart as her pup raised a weak snout and whimpered with recognition. The things these men had done…

She clamped her fist around the padlock and squeezed. It split open between her claws, mangled and useless. The door swung open.

The man with the hunting rifle stood, aiming with trembling hands. Irritated, the beast batted an arm behind her and smacked it out of his hands. Standing on her hind legs, she curled her claws around the edge of the door and pulled it all the way open.

"Please," the man said, "I'm sorry. We never meant to—"

The pup shuddered onto her paws, her whole body wracked with exhaustion. Angular ribs poked at the thin flesh of her chest. She glanced up at her mother, as if asking permission. The beast's face did not change.

"Please…"

Slowly, the pup turned her attention to the man. Her eyes lit up with hunger and she smiled. She took a single, shaking step forward, her claws scraping the floor of the cage as she dragged her paws. She shivered, shaking as though wet, and then her body stilled. Calmed.

She shot forward in a blur of shadow and the man's screams joined the howls of the creatures around him as she ripped into his throat.

(Moonlight.)

THERIANTHROPY

Leonard knew he was getting older – Christ, Janine insisted on *reminding* him enough – but old enough to be this hungover after two doubles of whiskey the night before? 'Fucking lightweight,' he grunted, drizzling a little splash of Jameson's into his coffee. 'You're a goddamn disgrace, Lenny.'

His head pounded as he rummaged in the kitchen cupboard for a frying pan and slammed it onto the hob. He winced, blood thumping his eardrums; one of these days, he was going to smash something. *Then* he'd have a headache.

'Janie!' he yelled, cracking two eggs into the pan and reeling back as a thick gob of oil spat up into his face. 'Come get your breakfast, you lazy drip!'

He stumbled across the kitchen and took a long glug of his hair-of-the-dog-infused coffee. He belched, spilling a little on his wrist. He barely noticed the burning. His whole body was tingling oddly, almost crackling. Putting the mug down shakily, he raised both hands and looked at his arms. Sinewy muscles bulged beneath paper-thin skin. He frowned. There was something strange about his arms – something laying over the skin, a thin layer of electricity like a caul of sizzling mucus – but he couldn't *see* it, not quite…

The frying pan popped loudly and he lurched back to the oven, his stomach swilling as it bounced against the walls of his gut. Quickly he dialled down the heat and whipped the pan off the hob.

'Janine, you cow!' he called. 'Get down here before I eat both of—'

He dropped the pan and doubled over. His throat seemed to turn inside out as his stomach threw a wall of foul-tasting acidic matter against his teeth. He retched and thick strings of gluey mucus oozed onto the tiled floor, slopping from his maw and drizzling over his stubbled chin.

'Ohh,' he moaned, rocking back onto his knees and awkwardly wiping his lips on the back of his wrist. He froze, his forearm hovering inches from his face. *There*. Finally, he put his finger on it.

All the hairs on his arm were standing on end. *Right* on end, almost buzzing with the thin fields of air trapped between them. Christ, how long had his arms been *this* hairy? Some of them were an inch long, some even more still. Jet-black, like the hair on his balding head – thankfully not grey, like the thatch of his chest and the spray of salt in his beard – and thicker than he'd realised, bunched together and shooting up out of his skin.

He groaned as another wave of nausea rushed up his throat, bending forward to vomit again. His knees shot apart and he threw up between them, spitting thick gobs of mucus onto the tiles when the rest had come up. A pale spray of fluid painted his ankles.

Thank Christ he hadn't embarrassed himself at the party like this. Oh, he was sure he'd embarrassed himself *somehow* – he usually did, and he never remembered – but he was confident he hadn't thrown up on anybody.

He leant against the cupboard behind him, pinching his nose and squeezing his eyes shut tight. His back itched – more hairs, standing up along the length of his spine? – and he could feel them prickling the back of his neck too.

Suddenly he rocked forward to retch again – and his eyes bulged in his skull as something lodged in his throat. A thick clump of something solid smashed into his neck and burned there.

Leonard panicked. He gagged, using every muscle in his throat to try and push the lump forward, but it was stuck. Blocking his windpipe. He couldn't breathe. Couldn't think. God, what the hell had he eaten?

His whole body crashed forward and he landed on his hands and knees, gawping at the tiles. His mouth opened wide, wider still, as though that would help the awful clot of bitter-tasting whatever-it-was to slide out. Oh, it felt odd. Hairy, almost. Tickling the tissue of his throat as it bulged and expanded in there. His chest heaved – wasn't enough – he was running out of breath, saw black clouds blooming at the edges of his vision – shit – *shit* – he wrenched the muscles of his stomach upward, spluttering with thin, flailing ropes of saliva tumbling from his gob—

There was a sensation of release, followed immediately by an enormous pain in his gullet, and then the lump shot out of his mouth and exploded onto the floor.

'Oh, god,' he moaned, drawing in ragged breaths and launching into an awful, wet cough as he sucked mucus and spittle back into his throat. Something had torn in his windpipe. 'Oh, god, Jesus…'

The thing on the floor had sunken into itself and it shivered lightly, coated in vomit and blood. A little mound of knotted, dark hair. *His* hair. But that was…

'Lovely,' Janine said from the kitchen doorway, her voice tinged with disgust.

Leonard looked up, his weight shifting onto his elbows. He saw a vague silhouette in the corner of the room and shook his head. 'I…' he tried, but his vocal cords were tangled and ruined. 'I…'

'I'm going back to bed,' Janine murmured. 'Sort yourself out, you prick.'

He moaned after her as she disappeared into the

hallway, listened absent-mindedly as she clomped up the stairs above him. He could feel his skin shivering, a dreadful warmth spreading across his muscles. He swung his arm into his face and looked.

'No…' he rasped. His arm was covered in vomit, but the hairs on his hand and knuckle were thickening, growing right before him. Five bolts of electric pain shot into the ends of his fingers and he yelped as the nails burst forward, ripping chunks of flesh with them as they narrowed into sharp, bony points.

He crumpled, his head hitting the floor. The hairball shivered in a dreadful pool of vomit, inches from him. Something at the party. Something had happened at the party.

No… *after* the party.

He remembered stumbling out of the function room into the cool air. The moon was a smoky orb of blue above him, bloated and obnoxious. He stumbled a little, giddily trampling a flowerbed along the edge of the path. Giggling, he staggered back onto the concrete and lurched into the road.

The thin husk of a bony tabby cat sat at his feet, looking sorrowfully up at him.

Leonard paused, looking down at the mangy creature. Its ears were pointed and bent back from its head, the leathery skin of which was tightly wound around a bulging skull. Its malnourished body was a spiral of angular ribs; patches of wispy fur thrust out of blistered, red-raw pores.

Hungrily, it mewled up at him.

For a moment a pregnant silence hung between them. Moonlight glittered off the cat's disc-like eyes and they shone brightly in its deformed skull. Tiny pointed teeth, mashed between a dry nose and a tangled white beard, formed an expression on the thing's face that was almost hopeful.

'You think *you're* hungry?' Leonard spat. He laughed, leering down at the underfed little beast. 'You oughtta try living on minimum wage for a month or two, fella.'

Then he lashed out and kicked the cat right in its bony chest, punting it across the road. There was an awful yelp and it tumbled over itself, clawing at the tarmac and skittering backward.

It had followed him home. He remembered stopping on the corner, looking back to see the lithe creature stalking him with its back arched, hackles raised.

Surely not, he thought now. Christ, *surely* that couldn't be it. It couldn't—

But he remembered. It had followed him right to the front door, only running away when he lurched forward and threatened to kick the bastard thing again. And as it had left, it had shot him one last look – and its eyes had shone so brightly…

He shrieked as his spine cracked suddenly,

smashing into his lungs and heart and wrenching him onto his belly. He turned his head, looked toward the oven door. Caught sight of his reflection in the greasy black glass and screamed.

His eyes bulged, doubling in size as he watched, a thick film of shining light cascading over his vision. His balding hair thickened, darkened, shooting out of his scalp, great hunks of hair ripping through the skin of his cheeks and jowls. He opened his mouth to moan and watched in horror as his gums split open, thick red tracks running onto his tongue as, one by one, every one of his teeth was shunted out of its place and fell clattering onto the tiles. New teeth, savage, pointed teeth, exploded from his ruined gums and shot chunks of blood into his mouth.

His body convulsed as his elbows bent inward, the bones cracking loudly. He tried to raise his arm – thick, black hair had become a blanket across his skin, and now he could feel the skin tearing, shredding itself open. He clawed at himself, digging sharp nails into the flesh and peeling. As the thick, black hair fell away ribbons of blood and pus seeped out of him and the layers of skin beneath were revealed – thin, leathery skin, covered in a much paler coat of mangy hair…

He tried to scream again, but his voice came out as a tiny, terrified mewl.

His stomach contracted suddenly and a thick clot of hair punched up into his throat, and Leonard could do nothing but hack and wheeze as it ripped at the cartilage of his neck.

On the counter above him, his coffee steamed softly.

GRAMPA MARROW'S HAT

Pip stepped toward the smouldering fireplace, his gaze shifting upward, drawn for the millionth time to the grainy black-and-white photograph on the mantelpiece, a bland family portrait in a marbled wooden frame.

Two boys and their father.

On the left, a younger version of Pip's father stood with his hands held before him, his hair neatly combed and his jacket and overcoat drawn up tight to his chin. In a shirt and waistcoat, the second boy stood with his hands stuffed in his pockets and a wicked grin on his face.

Behind them both, Grampa Marrow leaned forward with a hand on each young man's shoulder. He was an eight-foot-tall figure in a dark suit and a bowler hat, with a steely anger in his eyes and long, slender arms and legs. He looked like he had been stretched.

Pip shuddered as snow flurried at the window of the living room and the Christmas tree was gently impressed by the warm draft of the fire.

From behind him came the rustle of paper as something shifted in the small mound of gifts beneath the tree.

Early in the evening, Uncle Abel came into Pip's room with a small, brown cardboard box in his hand. He smiled as he crouched at the end of the boy's bed, the thick, salt-and-pepper flush of his moustache twisting into a cruel dark smile on his upper lip.

"Evening, champ," the big burly man said softly. Uncle Abel wore a thin white vest and bright, blood-red suspenders, a dark thatch of chest hair visible through the fabric. He smelled like mulled wine and tobacco smoke. "Now, I know you're excited for tomorrow, but I want you to make me a promise."

Pip nodded quickly. His mother had tucked him tightly into the duvet and he was curled up with his thumb pressed gently between his teeth; his head was just about all he could move.

"Good boy," Uncle Abel said. His eyes were a maudlin grey, slick black wires of hair greased back from a square knot of forehead. Almost gingerly, he laid the little cardboard box on Pip's bed, just out of the boy's reach, and leaned back to pluck a polished oak pipe from his trousers and light it up. This took a few moments, and as he put the pipe in his mouth and drew from it, he spoke again. "Christmas is a very happy time for us all. I understand that."

Pip beamed, withdrawing his thumb from his mouth and opening it to speak.

Uncle Abel held up a hand. "Christmas is a very happy time for *us all*," he repeated. "Not just you. You understand?"

Pip hesitated. He nodded, unsure what his uncle was getting at. The broad-shouldered beast puffed slowly at his pipe and his belt buckle glinted as it caught the glow from Pip's nightlight. The boy's room was small and plain, furnished only with a small bedside cabinet and an old school desk by the window. His toys were laid neatly on the sill in small boxes and jars, and his clothes hung from a bare iron rail in the corner.

Downstairs, he could hear his mother gently snoring above the low thrum of the television and the crackle of the fire in the living room.

"What I'm saying is, Mummy and I would like to spend some time together on Christmas morning," Uncle Abel continued. He tapped the little box on the bed. "And you're getting a little old to be bursting into our bedroom at six a.m., aren't you?"

The boy nodded slowly, disappointment rising in his chest.

"I knew you'd understand," Uncle Abel said, getting to his feet. He leaned over and ruffled the boy's messy red hair, grinning around the pipe jammed between his teeth. "I know things have been different since your daddy died, champ. I know he used to spoil you rotten at Christmas."

Pip said nothing. He tried not to think about Daddy; it made him cry. Uncle Abel didn't think boys should cry.

"Well, anyway, I want Christmas to be all about your mother, you understand? And you should want the same for her." Uncle Abel's face went hard. "Don't you?"

Pip nodded.

"Good boy. Open your present, champ. And don't you come knocking on Mummy's bedroom door tomorrow, okay? You let your uncle look after her for a little while, and when we're good and ready we'll come downstairs and spend Christmas all together. Like a family."

There was a bitterness in the way he said that, but Pip wouldn't understand it completely for a few more years.

Carefully, the six-year-old sat up in bed and reached across for the box. It was dusty, and the markings on its lid were faded, but he thought it might have been an old shoe-polish box. The lid was a struggle with his little hands, but he pried it off with a little grunt and looked inside.

The box was lined with thin brown tissue paper. Ten tiny lead figures lay moveless and dead in the slightly-damp confines of the box. Three of them held what looked like miniature sniper rifles, and one was lying prone with a chunky pistol in both hands. Their faces were missing.

"Oh, wow!" Pip grinned up at the beast towering above him. "Toy soldiers! Thank you, Uncle!"

Uncle Abel smiled thinly. "Daddy."

"Thank you, Daddy," Pip said quietly, poking his fingers into the box and picking up one of the soldiers – a little faceless lump of grey lead with a helmet and a bulky protective vest slung across his little leaden chest. "It's the best Christmas present I could have asked for."

"There's a good boy. Happy Christmas, champ," Uncle Abel said, squeezing the boy's shoulder. His heavy footsteps shook the floorboards as he moved to the door and left, closing it behind him.

Pip's excited smile dropped. He let go of the soldier and it dropped back into the box, falling dead among its comrades. Silently, he swung his legs out of the bed and slid onto the floor, then padded barefoot to the window.

Unceremoniously, he tipped the contents of the box into a greasy glass fishbowl on the sill, where the ten tin soldiers his uncle had given him joined three or four dozen more. His collection of lifeless army men, their faceless faces pressed against the glass, screamed silently as he picked up the bowl and carried it across the room.

Kneeling beside the bed, he tipped them all out and counted.

Fifty-two soldiers. Pip sighed quietly and started to put them all back in the bowl, the dull clunk of metal on glass booming like the crack of the gunshot that would kill each one. Fifty-two little dead lead men.

Just as many as he'd had at the beginning of the year.

Christmas morning came in a flurry of plump white snowdrops that beat at the narrow, single-glazed window, filling Pip's bedroom with spangles of swirling white. He lay in bed awake, watching the blizzard through teary eyes, desperate to leave his room and go down to see what Father Christmas had brought but terrified that the cruel spirit of winter that haunted their home would catch him first. Uncle Abel was the bitter spark of a blazing red fire that would leap from the hearth and burn the whole house down; he was a mountain of dark angry soil that had shovelled itself into the hole left by Pip's father and turned everything around it boggy and black. And Pip's mother had sunk, while the boy was forced to tiptoe around the edges of the mire and try not to get sucked in.

Gently, he slipped out of bed and walked silently across the bedroom. He could hear Uncle Abel and his mother in their own room down the hall, arguing quietly enough that he couldn't discern the words, only the bitter dreadfulness of them. It didn't matter what they were arguing about; she would come around and admit she'd been wrong. She always did.

Pip paused at the door, pressing his knees together as the urge to urinate swelled in his belly. He had made it till eight o'clock, though he had been awake since dawn and practically trembling with excitement since. Now he needed to go.

He cringed at a hard, loud *smack* from down the hall. The arguing voices went silent suddenly and fatally. Frozen at the door, Pip squeezed his eyes shut tight and waited. He wanted to burst in, to rip Uncle Abel away from his mother and drag him down the stairs. Maybe the hearth was already lit – he'd jam the man's big fat head into the fire and hold it there – then maybe it would all stop – maybe his mother would remember that Pip's father had once existed, and that Pip still did, and that *she* did too—

The boy's breath hitched in his throat as the awful silence from down the hall turned to a soft, repetitive grunting and the muffled thump of the bedframe against the wall. He thought he could hear his mother sobbing.

Anger flared in Pip's chest and he wrenched the door open, stumbling into the hall and heading blindly for the stairs. His need for the bathroom forgotten, he lurched past it and tumbled downstairs, leaving those awful sounds behind. Peeling strips of wallpaper watched him stagger through the decrepit hall and into the living room, where he stood in the doorway and stared in awe.

While the rest of the house was a shambles of broken wood and plaster, this room was decked in massive wreaths of tinsel and mad whirls of flickering electric lights. Deep red walls were bathed in the shifting, swelling glow of the lights and the snow at the windows patted softly on the glass, blistered sunlight refracting through each drop so that Pip felt he was underwater. Gold and glitter tumbled down the eaves of a marvellous, huge Christmas tree in the middle of the room, its branches proud and thick and a ring of needles scattering the floor beneath it. There were gifts galore, more than Pip had ever thought possible, all wrapped in thick, luscious paper and tied with ribbons that seemed to flutter as though there were a draft coming in from—

His eyes flitted to the hearth just in time to see something slither up it, a long black shadow slinking into the chimney flue before he could make out its shape. He gasped, stumbling backward and into the wall. His heart was beating a million miles a minute. Moments later, the logs in the hearth flared and the fire was lit and crackling, as though there had been nothing there at all. Perhaps there hadn't. He blinked.

The slamming of heavy footsteps upstairs yanked Pip back to the real world and he looked up, swallowing nervously before rushing to the living room door and pressing it closed. Something in the chimney or not, he would rather be in here than up there.

Slowly, he turned his face back toward the fireplace. Foamy sap drizzled from the chewed-up ends of logs as they burned, soot blooming across the back of a thin grille of iron mesh. Pip stepped closer, looking up toward the photograph on the mantelpiece. From behind the shoulders of two young men, a black-and-white Grampa Marrow in his dark suit and bowler hat leaned forward and looked down at him with those piercing eyes, two points of silvery-white in his narrow face.

Uncle Abel had put the picture up there when he'd moved in. Pip's father had seldom spoken of Grampa Marrow, but the boy knew that his grandfather hadn't been a very nice man. He had seen the scars across his father's back and knew that the crook in his nose had been the result of a childhood beating; Pip imagined both brothers had suffered equally, but perhaps where his father had been shaped into a warm, kind man who'd made it his duty to raise Pip better, Abel had been twisted into something cruel and cowardly, something that kept Grampa Marrow's spirit alive.

Something rustled loudly behind Pip and he

wheeled around, glancing down toward the source of the sound.

The gifts beneath the tree were still, though he could have sworn that something had moved.

He advanced, crumpling to his knees and digging his hands into the menagerie of moveless boxes and bulges. Upstairs, Uncle Abel tramped about like a demon. Pip ignored the sound and started to look at the tags. One for Abel. And another. Three addressed to his mother in Abel's handwriting, and a couple for both of them from neighbours and Uncle Abel's work friends.

Another for Abel. Two more for Pip's mother.

Softly, the boy sat back on his ankles and began to cry. Nothing from Father Christmas, and not a single present addressed to him. His father would have reminded him that Christmas wasn't supposed to be about the gifts – but where was Daddy now? Where was he?

Again, something rustled.

Pip's sobbing slowed and he looked up, his eyes puffy and wet. One of the gifts that he hadn't checked was balanced on the top of another, and as he watched, it tipped slowly, seesawing gently as though just moments ago something had poked it. It was oddly shaped, about half the size of a shoebox but circular on the bottom, with a smaller circle at the top so that it looked like somebody had sawn a cone in half and wrapped up the result; cautiously Pip reached forward and plucked it from the pile.

The paper was cold.

He flicked over the tag, which was damp at the edges like it had been sitting out in the snow, and beamed with excitement. *Phillip*, read a scrawled mess of soot-black handwriting, *Have a merry merry Christmas. K.*

Pip frowned as he wondered briefly who *K* could be, but before he could stop himself he had forgotten about it and was tearing through the paper. Scraps fluttered to the carpet around him as the firelight crackled at his back. He ripped open the package and marvelled curiously at the thing in his hands.

It was a velvet black bowler hat, the flocked material stiff and dusty, the rim chewed by age. It had clearly been worn – every day for years, it looked like – but there was no name printed on the inside, no tag. Just a tangle of sticky grey hair and a few spots of blood. Disgusted, Pip dropped the hat and clapped the dust off his hands, scrambling to his bare feet to get away from it. "What—"

From upstairs came the deafening racket of glass shattering. Pip's head shot up to the ceiling, his mouth falling open. Uncle Abel had smashed something again. In *his* room?

"No. No, please," he said, beginning to sob again. "I haven't done anything wrong…"

He rushed to the living room door, the hat forgotten, the boy's instincts telling him to get upstairs and stop Uncle Abel from destroying all his things before his brain could tell him that this was a very stupid idea. He belted for the stairs and lolloped up them, tears streaming down his face. Without hesitating, Pip grabbed the doorhandle and crashed into his bedroom.

He yelped as something razor-sharp ground into the sole of his bare foot, ripping flesh as it jabbed upward. He tumbled forward as warm pain flooded his leg, landing on his hands and knees on the floorboards. The door slammed shut behind him.

The floor was covered with glass. Shards as big as dinosaurs' teeth were scattered across the boards, and tiny sprinkles glittered between the cracks. His toy soldiers were littered among the wreckage, dozens of faceless lead corpses in the shattered ruins of their fishbowl home.

"No," Pip moaned, heaving himself to his feet and trying not to scream as the pain in his foot worsened. Snow beat angrily at the window, great storms of white pounding quietly on the glass, threatening to smash that too. Uncle Abel was nowhere to be seen. Pip looked down, awkwardly grabbing his ankle to get a better look at his foot. Dug into the soft flesh was a sliver of curved glass the length of a teaspoon. He pinched the end of it and closed his eyes. And pulled. "Oh…"

The glass unsheathed itself from his foot soundlessly and a warm spray of blood dashed his leg. He looked at the thing in his hand and saw that it was painted with a glossy sheen of red.

Agony swelled in his foot as it drunkenly returned to the floor. Pip felt dizzy. Had to get help. He turned back to the door, about to call out for his mother when his eyes snapped wide open and the words caught in his throat. Instead he gasped, almost choking on the bitterly cold air that he sucked in.

Grampa Marrow stood in front of the door and towered over him. He looked just the same as he did in the photograph, except his skin and clothes were see-through, made of a slowly-shifting fog that caught the white snowy light of the window and refracted it a million ways so that he cast thick splotches of glowing white onto the walls and the bed.

"You're dead," Pip whispered dumbly as he went to step backward, then froze remembering all the glass. "You can't be here, you're dead – and it's Christmas—"

Grampa Marrow leaned forward, just like he had done when the photograph on the mantelpiece was taken. His arms stretched toward Pip, his fingers impossibly long and bony, the papery skin of his hands flickering in shades of milky translucence. His suit was a slender well of shadow laid over his bones – oh, god, Pip could see his bones through his chest and the outline of his skull through his face – and his eyes were bright white points, silver discs in sunken sockets. His teeth flashed as he grinned wickedly and swiped at the boy.

Pip ducked and Grampa Marrow's arm whooshed through the air above his head. A great draft of wintery air ripped across the room with it, and all of Pip's toys crashed off the shelf and skittered over the floor.

The door slammed open suddenly and Uncle Abel crashed in, his face red and angry, his shirt half-buttoned. "What the hell is going on in here?" he yelled, lunging forward – and through Grampa Marrow's spindly torso as if the old man wasn't there at all.

"Can't you see him?" Pip screamed, pointing madly. Above them both Grampa Marrow grinned, reaching up to lift a ghostly bowler hat off his head and run his long, clawed fingers through the wisps of grey hair floating around his veiny scalp.

"You've finally cracked, boy, have you?" Uncle Abel seethed, smiling thinly. "Well, then, I know just how to set you right…"

Behind him, Grampa Marrow reached up with one arm and swiped his foggy fingers through the ceiling. The room shuddered as the plaster above them cracked and chunks of it began to rain down on the floorboards.

"What in fucking Christ—"

"The hat," Pip realised, looking up at the dusty

black bowler on the thin man's head.

"Oh, no, you don't, you little shit." Uncle Abel tried to grab him but Pip darted past, tumbling through the open door and back toward the stairs. He practically fell down them, almost tripping over his own feet as he rocketed into the living room. His foot throbbed painfully but he ignored it, the pain somehow numbed by a thick curtain of fear that had enveloped him. Loud, thudding footsteps followed him and he couldn't tell if they belonged to Uncle Abel or the ghostly figure of Grampa Marrow – or both – but it didn't matter, the hat was there on the floor, right there in a little heap of damp Christmas paper—

His chest went awful cold suddenly and he gasped. Everything slowed down. The snow lashing the windows seemed almost calm, sluggish, and the fire crackling in the hearth waned into a gentle pool of amber. He looked down.

Pip could see the very tips of Grampa Marrow's translucent fingers poking out of his chest and through the fabric of his pyjamas, the sharp nails moving in a slow, deliberate circle. His lungs seemed to shrivel up as a freezing lump of ice wedged itself between them, and he looked up to see the vicious old man gurning back down at him. "No," Pip gasped as Grampa Marrow twisted. Black spots clouded the boy's vision and his head pounded. "No…"

Two very solid hands slammed into his back

suddenly, shoving the boy onto the floor. "You little *fucker*!" Uncle Abel yelled, bearing down on him with all the weight of an angry bear. Gasping as breath returned to his lungs, Pip swiped blindly around him for the hat. His fingers found the thing and he grabbed it. Thick fingers twisted into his hair and Uncle Abel slammed a knee into the boy's back. "You quit your wriggling, you filthy little worm!"

Pip twisted his whole body around with every ounce of strength he had and slammed the stiff rim of the hat into his uncle's jaw. There was no real power in the blow but it was enough of a shock to loosen the man's grip on his hair for a moment. Screaming, Pip scrambled free of him and crawled toward the fire.

He hauled himself to his feet, leaving a little ragged trail of red behind him. The pain in his foot was incredible, but he managed to stand, leaning toward the hearth, glancing back one last time as he prepared to throw the hat into the fireplace.

Pip froze when he saw the look on Grampa Marrow's face.

His mouth had twisted itself free of the malicious smile that had pulled its corners up toward his silvery eyes, and now it was curled in a silent scream of terror. His eyes drooped wetly and the wrinkles in the glistening snowy spectre of his skin were furrowed with anxiety. He reached for Pip with both hands, desperately grabbing for the boy, trying to stop him.

Pip was in control, he realised. If he had the hat – the one thing tying Grampa Marrow's wretched soul to this Christmas day – then he had the power. For the first time in his life, he was in charge.

Uncle Abel lurched to his feet, his shoulders rippling with every furious breath that wracked his chest. Teeth gritted, he wiped spittle from his face and reached for his belt. "Happy Christmas, you little bastard," he grunted, stepping forward.

Pip looked from Uncle Abel to Grampa Marrow and smiled. He pinched the rim of the hat, hard, the fire bursting into a hungry rage of blue and orange behind him. A dreadful must rose into the boy's nostrils; he couldn't tell if it was coming from inside the hat or from somewhere else entirely. He twisted his hand.

The spirit understood. Somehow, it understood.

And it sunk down into Uncle Abel's chest in a flurry of claws and teeth, all the burning red filaments of the lights on the Christmas tree burning through its semi-visible skin as it bore forward and greedily ripped him open.

NIGHT

SONG

"Mandy!" Jess called, her voice thick with sleep. The sheets were tangled about her legs; drool glued her cheek to the pillow. "Do you have to play that thing right now? It's… oh, Christ, what is it—"

She twisted her body to look at the digital clock beside the bed and froze.

Mandy stared at her wide-eyed, gripping the sheets to her neck. Her face was pale, her cheek painted bloody with the soft red of the clock display. "I'm not," she whispered.

Grease and dust smeared the glass. A dozen stuffed weasels stood stiffly in the cabinet, each mounted on a varnished, reddish slab of wood. Glassy black eyes stared out into the store. The creatures' little stubby paws clutched before them as though prepared to scrabble at the glass anytime the little bell above the entrance jangled.

Jess didn't get the feeling it happened very often.

Most of the counters were covered in dust, and the only sign that anybody had come in and out at all was a track of footprints in the dirty shag carpet that went from the door to the cash register, doubled back on itself, then veered off at the door toward a small room in which she had glimpsed shelves and shelves of books. "Here, Mandy," she murmured, leaning forward to tap the glass. "Look at these hideous little fuckers."

The weasels looked blankly up at her, their whiskers oiled and stiffened, their snouts bared into awful little snarls. They were dressed in sharp, miniature suits and waistcoats – even the females, Jess noted, as though the taxidermist hadn't bothered to check downstairs – and one had a top hat and cane.

"Creepy," she shuddered, standing up. "Who'd buy them, eh, Mandy?"

Nothing.

"Mandy?" she hissed, looking about her. "Oh, for—"

Jess stuffed her hands into the pockets of her corduroy, puffing air out through her cheeks. The soft light from a clutter of reading lamps behind her glinted off the lenses of her reading glasses. Always disappearing, she thought, always bloody running off and leaving me talking into thin air – staring into the cold dead eyes of a fucking stoat…

A hunched shadow moved behind her. A brisk dark shape lilting across the walls.

Jess wheeled round, cocking an eyebrow. "Oh, hello," she smiled. She pointed at the cabinet. "I was just admiring these guys."

The owner peered across at her from behind a bank of typewriters and nodded curtly. He was an ancient husk of a man, drawn up in black pinstripes with a white goatee and tufts of silver fluff about his ears. His nose was like a bird's beak; he looked, she thought, like a sketch from a children's book she'd once read. The mean old farmer who liked to wave his shotgun at kids and drop-kick badgers. The old man sniffled wetly in her direction then disappeared again, dipping behind a tall oil portrait and vanishing altogether.

"Mandy?" Jess hissed again, stepping into the store and looking all around. She glanced toward an open doorway to the left and her eyes were drawn up, toward a laminated A4 sign with the words ART/INSTRUMENTS/MEMORABILLIA printed in a font that she was pretty sure was Comic Sans. And purple, too. An arrow pointed up.

Instruments.

"Of course," Jess sighed, and she headed for the doorway.

Amanda Rivers used to play the harp.

Past tense.

Distant past, it felt like. But then, everything before

the letter was 'distant' past. To think it had only been seventeen months since it had slipped through the letterbox was to remember that, by now, everything could have been so much better.

Mandy had always told Jess that she'd been sort of forced into it, that her father – the Swedish prodigy, the man himself – would rather have had her killed than see her pursue anything but music. Really, she'd always said, there'd never been any choice. She'd enjoyed playing football at school; doodling cartoons in her workbook; building tiny, crappy birdboxes in design tech. She could've done anything, been anything, but Daddy had made her a musician.

Really, Jess knew that her wife enjoyed the harp. Loved it, in fact. Why else would she have kept playing it even after her father had died? She wasn't the type to think of it as some way of honouring him, keeping him alive – it wasn't as deep as that. She was good at it, damn good, and she loved the music she made more than most things in the world. When they had moved to their little Birmingham apartment, she had brought the harp with them: a plain, cherry-wood Salvi that took up half the lounge and cast long, jaunty shadows on the walls. And she played it most days, played the softest, warmest music that Jess had ever known. Mandy Rivers wasn't a cook (she could burn a lasagne at twenty paces) and while Jess wiped down the counters in the kitchen and stirred at the hob she would listen to Mandy playing in the next room, sometimes remembering old pieces she had learned under her father's tutelage – Salzedo, Tournier, Naderman – and sometimes crafting music on the fly, letting her fingers do the talking, sitting with her eyes closed for anywhere between twenty and eighty minutes and just letting her very soul flow through her and out into the space that only the two of them could ever know. They knew the walls were thin, and that the neighbours could probably hear it too, but somehow they managed to forget that. When there was music, it was their music.

The music stopped when the letter came. So did the sex. And the warmth of their home, and the conversation and laughter and happiness… and the hope.

The harp went into the skip along with an unused crib and three cans of yellow paint, and in the next few months the room they'd planned to use as a nursery became an oversized storage closet, with a spare bed in which Jess slept when they argued.

It was an arse to lug the thing up the stairs to the apartment, but between them they finally managed to heave it through the front door and into the lounge. It stood right where the Salvi had, and Jess stepped back as Mandy began to peel off the bubble-wrap flesh of the thing, pressing her knuckles to her hips and glancing up at the wall. There they were, the same long shadows, but there was a softer curve to them now. She bit her lip and looked anxiously at Mandy.

"You like it?"

Mandy ripped off the last of the bubble-wrap and stood back, joining her wife in the doorway. The living room was cramped, much of the wall space taken up with books and board games, but the harp didn't overfill the remaining space like Jess had thought it would.

"I love it," Mandy grinned, and when Jess glanced in her direction she saw a childlike wonder in the older woman's eyes that she hadn't seen in seventeen months, that she had missed so badly. "Thank you. Oh, thank you so much."

Jess wrapped an arm around Mandy's waist and they kissed. Then she pulled away and gestured to the instrument. "Play something. Please. Anything you like."

Mandy clapped her hands together, something akin to glee pushing her cheeks up toward her eyes. Jess moved around her and settled on the couch, butterflies creeping out of the nest in her stomach and batting their wings about its acidic walls. This could be it, she thought. This could save their marriage, or it could be the very last straw. It could destroy them. It all depended on the very first note that Mandy plucked.

"Come on," Jess said eagerly, "please."

Mandy moved to the harp, running a hand across its neck. Long, slender fingers danced lightly across the tuning pins.

It was an old, battered thing, chipped mahogany filled in and refinished in places. Twenty-two strings, strings which the hunched old owner of the antiques store had assured them were freshly tuned. Intricate carvings in the wooden, slanted heart-shaped frame of the thing had largely faded or been misshapen by the years, but Jess could just make out the figures of dozens of tiny people crawling up the wood, men and women beating their way to the top, almost clawing at each other to reach the polished crown of the thing.

Slowly, Mandy positioned herself on the dark, cushioned stool Jess had dug out of the storage room. The sole of her left foot perched gently on the harp's pedals, slim paddles of beech poking out from beneath the instrument. It was taller than her now, arcing up from her shoulder and crashing down again into the floor. She drew in a breath. Jess realised that she'd been holding hers, and gently let it go.

Mandy closed her eyes. Splayed her hands into wide fins, then popped the knuckles one by one and settled into the instrument. It was like something physically dropped her from a great height and she was not hurt by it, but relieved; and then she played.

The first thing she plucked was a seventh chord.

Jess grinned, entirely enamoured by the music that followed, and when Mandy finally opened her eyes half an hour had passed. She looked at Jess and smiled, and for a moment the forty-five-year-old woman looked like she had all the strength and youth of a child. Jess felt that she'd dropped a good decade, too, just sloughed it off like a snake shedding its skin.

Jess stood, moved to her wife and pressed her hands to Mandy's cheeks, gently wiping away tears. She had been crying too and for a moment they stayed there, their foreheads pressed together, sobbing gently while the notes rang in their ears.

Then wordlessly Jess took her wife by the hand and led her to the bedroom, and afterward they slept better than they had in a year and a half.

It was a full week before the horror began.

It was three forty-nine in the morning when the music awoke them.

Mandy had played the harp for some time after work every day since they'd bought it, songs and exercises coming to her as easily as though she had never stopped, and the notes and chords that flowed from her seemed to fill every room in the apartment with a kind of light that had faded, recently, replenishing the dull glow of their evenings together. The music was kind, and at times frantic and explosive, others melancholy and slow.

It never sounded like it did right now.

They crossed the bedroom together, Mandy in her knickers and socks, Jess in the polar bear pyjamas she'd gotten last Christmas. The door was closed, and the notes that passed muffled through the wood were jangly and unpleasant, smashed together violently and ripped apart again as whoever was playing the harp slapped madly at it with hands that, it seemed, had been quite broken by severe blunt trauma.

As Jess reached for the doorhandle Mandy whispered, "Hold on," and darted away, dipping into the laundry basket at the foot of the bed and withdrawing a dark jumper. She shrugged it on and nodded, and Jess twisted the handle and pushed.

The music continued as they stepped into the dark hall, tiptoeing and avoiding the boards that creaked the worst. Jess had been fitting a new curtain rail in the bathroom and as Jess passed the little pile of tools and folded, yellow cloth they had yet to hang, she bent down and grabbed the electric drill they'd been using. Glancing back at Mandy she brandished it like a bulky pistol and nodded. You all right?

Mandy nodded back confidently. Nope, not at all not one bit.

The music built to a tuneless crescendo as they approached the lounge doorway, shadows long on the walls. Jess felt something fumbling for her hand and nearly jumped out of her skin, then realised it was Mandy's clutching fingers and grabbed them, squeezing them as encouragingly as she could. An angry splintering of low bass notes was punctured by a dozen tiny riffles of high, piercing strings. Three, Jess thought, flexing her fingers around the drill and praying there was some battery left in it. Two. One…

She burst into the lounge and slammed her elbow into the light switch, thrusting the electric screwdriver in the direction of the harp and gritting her teeth in anticipation. Right behind her Mandy tumbled in, both her fists raised like those of a boxing hare.

The music had stopped.

There was nobody at the harp. The strings weren't even vibrating, though the echoes could still be felt on the air.

Jess lowered the drill. "I'll check the kitchen," she said, despite the fact that, to move from the lounge to the kitchen, the intruder would have had to come right past them. All Jess had felt was a cold blast of air, and that she simply attributed to the fact that she had crashed into the room like a bull.

They looked around the house for a solid forty minutes, checking every cupboard, every nook. Jess checked the front door was locked – it was – and eventually they decided that the music must have come from outside somewhere.

It must have.

Mandy didn't play the harp for a couple of days after that. It stood alone in the lounge, the strings slowly winding themselves out of tune, the polished wooden frame gathering tiny amounts of dust. The ornate carvings up the curved surface of the harp's that wrapped around its knee and snaked over the neck seemed to writhe and twist as the light from the window played upon them, so that it looked like the dozens of crawling, climbing men and women were pulling at each other in their frantic journey across the instrument.

In a week they had forgotten about the strange sounds of that night, and Mandy returned to the harp quite cheerfully. Jess was thrilled to see her happy again, to hear that music again, and only hoped that it would last awhile. She had missed it. Missed her. Had honestly thought that they would never feel in love again, but here they were.

It was no baby, but it was something.

She and Mandy had met late in their lives. By the time they came to considering applying for IVF treatment, Mandy was forty-two – right on the edge of 'too old' to be eligible. And at the time that hadn't been a problem, not at all, for thirty-seven-year-old Jess had wanted to have the baby.

It wasn't their fault the application had been

rejected. They'd done nothing wrong; that was just life. The problem was…

Oh, god, the problem.

Well, a part of the problem was that they were too old. By the time they'd appealed the decision, looked elsewhere, decided that Mandy could carry the baby – it was too late. Mandy was forty-three. Private IVF cost far too much for them to even consider, but they did consider it, and were rejected again. Mandy was too old to carry, by their standards, and as for Jess…

The problem.

The problem was called Nina.

Mandy's eyes snapped open to the sound of jangling harp strings.

The bedroom was dark, the moonlight coming in through the slit between the curtains doing little to illuminate anything. Jess was a vague shape wrapped in coils of bedsheet, a soft crescent of hair sticking up from the side of her head and quivering softly as she snored.

Mandy lay there for a few moments, staring at the back of her wife's head as she listened to the dark. The harpsound was unmistakeable; she could recognise each note, picture each sting twanging dreadfully, roughly, as it was played; could almost feel them buzzing against her fingers. Somebody was in their house. Somebody was butchering her instrument.

"Jess," she hissed, gently gripping the woman's shoulder and shaking it a little. "Jess, wake up."

Jess was too far gone, her mouth open, her closed eyelids fluttering gently as she twitched and jerked through whatever dream she was having. Deep asleep and content.

Mandy grunted and slipped out of bed, almost more annoyed than afraid. This had happened three times now, and she was almost entirely confident that by the time she reached the lounge it would have stopped. There'd be nobody there, and the harp would be still.

Either somebody was driving past their apartment at the same time every night playing the most obnoxious music through their car stereo, or she was going insane.

She grabbed the glass of water from her bedside cabinet and downed it quickly, curling her fingers tightly around the empty thing as she stood. She'd never glassed anyone before – and she really quite liked this glass; it had flamingos on it – but it was all she had to hand, and she was quite sure there'd be nobody to smash with it anyway.

"All right," she murmured, crossing the bedroom quietly. "Let's get this over with, shall we?"

She moved silently through the flat, gripping the glass so hard that she wondered briefly if it might just shatter in her hand. The awful tuneless wailing of the harp echoed around her, drowning out the creaking of the boards beneath her feet, drowning out the pumping of blood in her ears and the sharp, hitched breaths that escaped her throat. I'm not afraid, she thought, I'm not afraid. I'm not. But she squeezed the glass and raised it like a weapon nonetheless. Just in case.

The second she turned the corner into the lounge, the music stopped.

She stared at the harp, her mouth open a little, her eyes wide and frightened. "Oh my god," she whispered.

There was a man perched on her stool, his body translucent so that she could see the skirting board through his stomach; he seemed to be made of a thin, grey mist, his clothes too, not a shred of colour to his suit or face. His eyes were bright white points in the sunken pits of his skull; his cheeks were sallow, his neck long and wrinkled like the neck of a turtle. He was completely bald, and the hands pressed to the body of the harp were long and slender, the nails perfectly sharp like claws. He wasn't real, couldn't be. But he was looking right at her.

"Who—" she started, but the moment she began he disappeared, flickering out of existence like a dying lightbulb. One moment he was there, his wiry old body bent around the harp jammed into his shoulder, and the next there was nothing there at all.

Mandy swallowed. She had dropped the glass, she

realised, and it rolled slowly around her right foot on the carpet. The image of the man was gone, but the drilling white points of his eyes still burrowed into her.

"You're just tired," she said quietly, laying a hand over her eyes and breathing slowly. That was all. She hadn't been sleeping; she was tired. She'd imagined it all. In fact, though she could feel quite distinctly the solid creases of her palm, though she knew that she was awake right this second, the past few minutes had passed by in such an indescribable haze that she might have been asleep until just a second ago. Maybe it had all been a dream. Had she sleepwalked before? She didn't think so, but there was a first time for everything.

By the time she crawled back into bed and tugged the sheets up to her neck, she had almost forgotten the dead man's face.

Most evenings over the next couple of weeks, Mandy played for at least a couple of hours; they'd had an arrangement, until recently, that Jess would happily cook if Mandy helped her with the washing up after, but now she barely even took a ten-minute break to eat. The moment her fork hit the empty plate Mandy was up again, moving across the lounge to pluck gently at the harp, and by the time Jess was finished her wife was so deep in the music that it seemed a shame to ask her to step away from it again.

They hadn't had each other in a week. And that was okay – Christ, they'd gone far longer than that without and it hadn't meant anything – but Jess felt that it was different this time. "What, then?" she snapped to herself, buried up to her wrists in the washing-up bowl. The soft beautiful thrum of the harp rang all around her, consuming and bitterly unkind. "Are you jealous of a harp, now? Grow up, Jessica."

But it wasn't jealousy. It was certainty; slowly, surely, Mandy was forgetting about her.

Every weekend, Jess made the trip to visit Nina at her foster parents' home in Leeds.

She and Roy had been together for four years, and in that time he had taught her pretty much everything there was to know about domestic violence. As far as she could remember it had been six months of contented, enamoured bliss followed by a solid three and a half years of terror, of trying desperately to leave – and of course, every time she tried to he would cry, and the emotion would be so dreadfully real that she had to stay – and somewhere in all that time she had his child, and that had only made it harder to leave. Sometimes, when she was feeling particularly cynical, she thought that Roy had impregnated her quite deliberately to keep her from leaving, but even he couldn't have been so malicious. Surely not.

Surely not.

She kissed Mandy goodbye on Saturday morning and headed out to the car, pulling on her scarf and zipping up her parka, her breath blooming visibly in front of her mouth as the cold air struck her hard. Mandy had come on these trips with her until the letter, and the three of them – Mandy, Jess and Nina – had been like a little family of their own, and whenever the two of them could steal the girl away from her foster parents for a few hours they had a lot of fun. They laughed. If not for Nina, Jess often thought, she and Mandy would never have considered trying for a baby of their own.

If not for Nina, their application might have been successful.

Before she was ten feet from the front door, Jess heard the muffled notes of the harp drifting out through the wood. She paused by the car, closed her eyes, and breathed deeply.

To her, Nina was the other half of everything. The one good thing that had come out of her time with Roy. She had struggled with the idea of keeping the baby – her parents had been all for it, oblivious to Roy's treatment of her but above all else strictly anti-abortion – and in the end, really, she'd been glad that she was so much in their thrall, for she couldn't imagine a world where Nina didn't exist. She was beautiful, kind, so unlike her father that it was a miracle.

Then, of course, Roy had tried to kill them both. Jess didn't like to remember that, but now that she was making these trips on her own – driving two hours there and another two back home every Saturday, by herself – she found it hard not to think about it all.

To her, Nina was the other half of everything. And to Mandy, Nina was A Child By A Previous Relationship and the reason Jess was ineligible for IVF treatment. The reason they couldn't have a family of their own.

And that was just the way things were.

Mandy closed the door and moved swiftly back into the lounge, unthinking, drawn there by some invisible string tied around her hands. Before she could stop herself she had sat on the stubby little stool beside the harp and pressed her fingers to the strings, and then her eyes were closed and the next half hour – the next hour; the rest of the morning – disappeared into a blossoming cloud of wonderful, inevitable noise.

When she woke up, her fingers were bleeding.

"Ooh," Mandy hissed sharply, reeling back from the harp as she noticed the warm, tingling pain spreading across the pad of each finger. She looked down at her hands; she was cut, the flesh scored all over, thick fat beads of blood pulsing from the shallow dips in her skin and twisting into thin rivulets of red. The strings of the harp were painted with it, smeared with it, bright blood-red cords pulled tight as though drawn up out of the disembowelled belly of some poor creature and shining wetly in the light.

A spattering of blood on the carpet around the harp.

"Shit," Mandy said, wiping her hands on her trousers and cringing as the denim aggravated each cut, shooting fresh bolts of pain up into her hands. She stumbled up from the stool and went to the kitchen, rinsing her hands in cold water until the blood had stopped. Fixing up the worst injuries – those on her thumbs and index fingers, she found – with plasters, she scrambled in the cupboard for a batch of cleaning products and returned to the harp.

The front door started to open as she was wiping blood off the strings. Mandy's head shot up, terrified, and she looked out into the hall to see Jess coming in, unzipping her coat. "Hiya, honey!" Jess called.

"Shit," Mandy whispered again. Tucking the bloody cloth into her pocket, she lurched into the doorway, leaning on the frame with one hand and hoping that her body blocked the awful sight from view.

Jess looked up, unlacing her boots. "You all right there?" she grinned.

"Hey," Mandy said, "you look cold. You fancy a bath?"

Jess slipped out of her boots and stepped forward, smiling. "I'd like that, actually," she said softly. "Are you planning on joining me?"

Mandy smiled unconvincingly. "If you'll have me," she said, swallowing. "How about you head through and run it for us, and I'll be there in a few—"

"Mandy, your hands," Jess said sharply. "God, your trousers – what happened to you?"

"Nothing," Mandy said, shifting her body as Jess tried to look past her. "Come on, then, let's—"

"Oh my god," Jess said, pushing past her into the lounge. "Mandy!"

When Mandy turned to look, the harp seemed to have gotten even more bloody than she'd left it. Every string was drenched, and the spattering on the floor had followed her out into the hall, a little trail of red dots in the carpet betraying her every movement. In the light coming through the window she saw dozens of flakes of broken skin floating softly on the air, many of them tinged with crimson.

Jess turned back to her, reaching for Mandy's hands. She snatched them away instinctively.

Jess shook her head. "How long were you playing?" she whispered. "Christ, Mandy, I've been out all day. Tell me you've not been there since I left."

Mandy didn't have an answer. She remembered Jess leaving, and then…

"Oh, god, really? You haven't eaten? You've just

been…"

Mandy blinked, tears forming in her eyes.

"Mandy, what's going on?"

"I don't… I'm sorry, Jess, I don't know. I don't know what happened to me, I don't… it's like one minute you left and the next you're back and all the space in-between is… is… is gone. I… I don't even remember playing."

Jess reached again for Mandy's hands, held them softly. "Okay," she said. "Okay. That's fine. I'll tell you what. Let's get you into some new jeans, get these ones in the wash. I'll clean up the floor, and you go get some water on these fingers."

Mandy looked down, saw that the cuts she hadn't fixed up with plasters had begun to well with blood again. It was on Jess's hands now, too.

"And let's put the harp in the storage room, shall we? Just for a couple of days."

Red flares exploded in Mandy's vision. She gripped Jess's hands tight and snapped her eyes upward, her heart suddenly pounding. "No," she said flatly.

Jess cocked an eyebrow, trying to withdraw her hands; she couldn't. "Mandy, what are you… let go of me."

"It's not going in storage."

"Okay!" Jess snapped. "Fine, just – Christ, Mandy, you're hurting me!"

She jerked her hands free and stepped back, shaking

her head.

Mandy's eyes were on fire, burning with a ferocious intensity that Jess hadn't seen before – not in those eyes, at least – and she backed up to the wall, suddenly afraid.

"Do your own cleaning up," she said bluntly, and she stepped shakily past Mandy into the hall, bolting to the bathroom.

"I'm sorry," Mandy sniffled, her throat heaving violently as she began to sob. "I'm so sorry."

But she couldn't rip her eyes off the harp, and the thick gluey threads of blood drooling down the strings.

When the sounds of the harp woke Jess they were different than they had been on other nights – softer, far less deliberate – and she wondered if it could possibly be that she was hearing them from the spare room, rather than the bedroom; perhaps the door was made of a thicker wood, perhaps…

She crept out of bed wordlessly, hoping beyond hope that the playing had woken Mandy too and that the two of them would meet in the hallway. They would share a knowing, terrified glance, reach for each other's hands, face it together. Reconcile.

The hallway was empty, and Jess walked alone toward the sound. She heard a faint snoring as she passed the bedroom door and momentarily considered ignoring the music altogether and crawling into bed with her wife. Argument be damned, she needed her – they needed each other, that had always been true and there was no reason it shouldn't be just because they'd had a little spat – but no. Mandy was peacefully asleep, and Jess was… well, curious, more than anything.

It was no passing car blasting obnoxious music. She knew the next-door neighbours weren't particularly musical – in fact, they might have been in France this week anyway – and the takeaways beneath the apartment were all closed this early in the morning.

There was somebody in the lounge. Not playing the harp, but stroking it gently, running their fingers along the strings and sending such delicate, insignificant notes into the air that really their fingers must have been brush-light.

Jess swallowed and stepped into the lounge, not bothering to turn on the light.

The flickering apparition of an old, grey man crouched beside the harp, running the fingers of one translucent hand up and down the longest string. Jess stared. She could see right through him, his body formed of particles of mist. His eyes were half-closed as a sick kind of pleasure twisted his face, but she could see that they were bright and white and shining.

As she watched, he licked one string from bottom to top, drawing the tip of his grey, semi-visible tongue up it like a dog deciding whether to masticate an old bone or toss it into the dirt.

He saw her – or she felt that he must've, though his blank, white eyes barely moved – and smiled.

"I can taste her," he whispered, his rasping voice like the soft, wet sounds of frozen weeds pulled from gravel.

Jess backed out of the lounge without a word and returned to the spare room, already sobbing before she slumped into the narrow bed and squeezed her eyes helplessly, hopelessly shut.

"I think we should get rid of it," Jess said calmly, slugging milk across the little mound of cornflakes in her Tasmanian Devil bowl. Behind her, Mandy stood with her back to the counter, sipping softly from a mug of coffee. The smell was delicious.

The plasters had been taken off, and the pads of her fingers were chipped and white. The heels of each hand were bruised. She said, "Why? I like playing it."

Jess chucked the milk back in the fridge and turned to face her. "We can get you another harp. Any other harp. That one… I think there's something wrong with it, Mandy. I think you think so, too."

Mandy said nothing. She took another sip, wincing as the hot ceramic pressed against her cuts.

Jess pushed her reading glasses up her nose and grabbed her bowl, heading to the drawer for a spoon.

"Tell me you've had a decent night's sleep since we bought it," she said, shutting the drawer just a little too hard. "Some nights it… plays itself, and other nights I'm so afraid it will that I can't get a wink, Mandy. And last night…"

No, she thought. Don't tell her about the man. It's too much. Too much, and you probably imagined it anyway.

"Last night it did it again," she said, "and I think it's doing something to you, too. The way you couldn't stop playing it yesterday… god, Mandy, I don't know if that was you or it, but I don't like it."

"So you want me to stop playing?" Mandy said, her voice low and distant. Jess looked; her eyes were on the floor, the steam from the mug obscuring her face.

"No," Jess said, "not for anything in the world. You know I love to hear it, and I love how happy it makes you, I just – god, I don't know. I don't know if this one is…"

Haunted, she thought. But it can't be, that's ridiculous.

"I don't know if it's right," she said finally. "We could go into town. Maybe on Thursday night, if the shops are open late. Do they still do that? Is that still a thing? Or at the weekend, if not. We'll get you a nice one. I could ask for an advance from work – we could sell this one, try and sell it back to the guy from the antiques store, even – we might lose a little, but…"

Mandy was looking at her. Her eyes were dull and cold. A tiny river of coffee had spilled over the side of the mug and was running into the palm of her hand, squeezed into the creases. It must have been burning her, but she didn't seem to notice. "The one shred of happiness I've found," she whispered, "and you want to take it away from me?"

Jess blinked. "I'm not… the one shred?"

Mandy said nothing.

"Are you saying I don't make you happy?" Jess said, suddenly feeling very small.

Nothing.

"Mandy, please—"

"I could be so good," Mandy breathed. "I could be so damn good at it, Jess. And you… you want to stop me? You want to get in the way of something I enjoy, just because I got a bit involved? Have you ever seen a guitarist's fingers, Jess? Hm? Cut to ribbons, aren't they?"

Jess shook her head. It wasn't Mandy's fingers, it never had been – it was the look in her eyes when she'd been caught cleaning up the blood. It was the vacant stare whenever she wasn't playing, it was the way she didn't even look at Jess anymore.

It was the ghostly grey man who'd been licking her blood off the strings.

"Let's just put it in the storage room," Jess begged. "For a day. A few days, maybe. Just while we're looking for a different one. Please, Mandy. Please."

"You think I'll forget all about it, don't you?" Mandy said, slamming her mug down on the counter. Coffee spilled everywhere as she lurched forward, pointing a shaking finger. "Like you hoped I'd forget my dream of having a family the moment it turned out we couldn't."

"Our dream," Jess whispered.

"Your fault it didn't work out," Mandy spat hatefully, "and then you gave up on it all, and prayed I'd forget and give up on it too so we could keep living our tiny little lives in this tiny little flat, and now you want me to forget about this too so we can keep just… plodding on!"

Jess didn't know what to say. Her fault. It was her fault it hadn't worked out. She'd known that for months, spent most days trapped in a little well of guilt she'd dug for herself; she'd known that Mandy must have blamed her, too, but to say it out loud…

"I've got to go to work," Mandy said. "You can have the car today, I'll walk."

As she crossed the kitchen, Jess reached out to touch her arm, to stop her. "Please, Mandy, listen to me. This isn't you, you're not like this. That thing… it's doing something to you."

Mandy yanked her arm loose and stormed out of the kitchen. "Fine!" she yelled. "Put it in storage, see if it'll make a difference."

Jess heard the rustling of Mandy's coat and her footsteps in the hall as she tramped to the front door and swung it open.

"Because I'll tell you something," she called, "it's not the music that's made me like this, Jessica, it's you. It's all your fault."

The door slammed behind her and Jess fell into the countertop, gripping it with both hands as she doubled over and sobbed, loudly, violently, wishing for all the world they'd never gone into that damned shop.

When Mandy came home she was apologetic. Infinitely, passionately apologetic. They held each other for a long time and Jess pressed her face into her wife's shoulder, crying softly into her coat.

They talked about it in the lounge, neither one of them able to look into the empty space where the harp had been. It lay on its side beneath the bed in the storage room, tossed gently under a thick linen sheet. Mandy was totally different than she had been that morning, and Jess supposed she had had eight hours to think about it all, to put the pieces back together and finally make sense of them.

Or she's just had a few hours away from it, she thought, and it has stopped doing whatever it was doing to her.

They spoke about finding a different harp. About

taking a trip to the coast the next weekend, maybe finding a little time for each other. Mandy told her that she'd never meant those things, not really. Jess said that was fine, it was understandable, it was a pressurised environment and…

Well. It didn't matter, not really. They both knew she was the reason their application had been rejected. That she was the reason they couldn't have a family. And whether it was hanging in the open or not, the fact remained.

And a part of her did wish Mandy would forget about playing the harp, just for the tiniest flash of a second. Just so she would never have to hear that music again.

After they had talked they kissed, deeply, and for the first time in a long time Mandy cooked dinner. They ate on the couch, both of their bodies turned slightly away from that dreadful empty space nearby, and for hours they watched telly and held each other close, and everything felt okay.

Everything felt so close to okay.

At three forty-nine in the morning, Jess opened her eyes. Mandy's arm was hooked softly around her waist, the sheets cocooning them both in a warm huddle. The radiator had been set to come on at three for half an hour, and the residual heat blossomed pleasantly across the room.

There was music. Lilting, out-of-tune music, bold spangles of it throbbing through the wall.

"Mandy, are you—"

"Yes."

"We have to get rid of it," Jess whispered, squeezing her eyes shut as she reached for Mandy's hand. She was exhausted, her head pounding, her whole body wracked with tiredness. She had barely slept at all the last few weeks and she was feeling it. "There's something wrong with it. We can't have it in the house."

And she couldn't, in good conscience, sell it to anybody else, but they would cross that bridge in the morning.

"Mandy?" she said quietly. Mandy's arm snaked away as she sat up, listening.

"It's in the storage room, right?" Mandy said. Her face was splashed with moonlight, her chest heaving gently.

"Yes."

"I'm going to take a look."

"Mandy, you know what you'll see, it's not worth—"

"I'm going to take a look."

She straightened her body and climbed out of bed, tugging on a shirt as she crossed the room.

"Mandy, please," Jess hissed, rubbing her eyes.

"Please don't go. Stay here with me. Please."

"I'll only be a second."

Mandy left the room and crept quietly into the hall.

Glancing toward the storage room, she saw that the door was closed, that it was how they'd left it. Still, the music wasn't coming from the storage room.

Silently she turned toward the lounge and padded across the carpet, heading toward the plinky-plonky awful sound. Briefly she closed her eyes and drew in a hesitant breath, pausing outside the doorway. She didn't want to look, didn't want to see—

But she had to.

She stepped forward and across the threshold, her eyes opening and snapping immediately toward the harp. The music stopped; the grey, spindly shape bent across its body flickered and disappeared. The white discs of its eyes sizzled in the air and died, a ghostly afterglow burning out. When she blinked, those two bright points burned the black space behind her eyelids like two dull purple flames.

The harp was still and quiet. In the bedroom she could hear faint snoring; Jess was so tired, bless her. Mandy knew that she'd been different, lately, that she'd been overwhelmed, gotten carried away, and she knew that – as much as she was convinced there was something about the harp, as much as she had seen it – it was still just her. Just her, lost in the music.

Her fault. Like it was her fault they'd waited too

long for IVF. Her fault she and Jess had grown so distant lately.

"I'm so sorry," she whispered, moving slowly toward the harp. Tomorrow they would put it away again, and make sure it was out of the house before they went to bed. Sometime, she would get another one. Probably have to wait until next payday, or the one after even, but she could do that. The two of them had other things to work out before she let herself get carried away again. Things could be so much better with a little time.

Without thinking, she stood beside the harp and ran her fingers across its neck, letting the smooth, chipped-and-filled-in wood brush her palm. The little carved figures seemed to dance in a mad ring around the instrument's body, their shallow carcasses forever arranged in a position that seemed fluid and mobile despite their moveless, dead shape.

"Whatever you are," she whispered, almost tempted to play it again, "I'll be glad to see the back of you."

She turned, pulling away from the harp to move across the room.

Something twanged loudly and she felt warmth lash her wrist, cried out a little as she looked down. A bright red arc of blood jetted from the flesh of her forearm where the string had smacked it, cutting deep. She clutched at her arm and stumbled back, looking up in terror at the thing. "What the—"

Another string snapped at the top with a violent tonk and coiled like a snake, twisting its razor-thin body into a spiral, a spring—

Mandy yelped as the string darted forward with a crack! and rapped her fingers, slicing through skin and drawing more blood. She tried to back away, wide-eyed, but the first string snapped forward and curled around her bloody wrist, tightening around the bones and yanking her forward. Some invisible shape kicked the stool forward and she tumbled, landing upon it as the second string punched into the knots of her hair and twisted, pulling her closer.

"No," she said, "no, please…"

"Play," whispered a voice in her ear, and she knew without looking up that those two flaring white eyes had reignited in the dark above her.

Soft grey light filtered into the bedroom as Jess blinked herself awake, a soft crust falling from her eyes as she yawned. "Mandy," she murmured, "are you awake?"

Nothing. Just the soft chirruping of the birds outside the window and the mutter of cars on the street below the apartment. Gently she sat upright, looking toward the clock on the bedside cabinet. A little after seven, and almost completely light.

"Mandy?"

Jess patted the empty space beside her, suddenly

registering the soft, musical notes of the harp tilting through the bedroom door. Not the messy, jangled ruin of half-song that had woken her up in the middle of the night but a dreamy, beautiful piece she recognised as one of Mandy's favourites.

"No," she moaned softly, starting out of bed and across the room, her legs weak. "Oh, Mandy, no…"

She burst into the living room and saw Mandy at the harp, weeping and red-faced. Her fingers worked delicately, strumming in perfect rhythm as she sobbed, her eyes raw and dull from lack of sleep, her hair and face a mess. A spider-web of dried blood crisscrossed her forearm. "Help me," she breathed, her fingers working without consent, playing wonderfully despite the terror in her eyes. "Please, Jess – I can't stop, I can't – help…"

Jess took a step back, clamping a hand over her mouth. One of the strings had snapped loose of the frame and buried itself in Mandy's wrist, and as she played it twitched and jerked as though working the tendons and joints of the poor woman's knuckles. There was another dug into the meat of her thigh and it bent and swayed as her feet moved lithely over the pedals.

"Mandy, what's going on?" Jess said, trying desperately not to scream. She took another step back, moving through the door into the hall.

"Don't leave me!" Mandy shrieked suddenly, and

Jess noticed that a third string, sharp as razor-wire and coiled like a serpent, was pointed directly at her weeping right eye. As she shook her head it followed; one wrong move… it said.

"I have to get something," Jess said breathlessly.

"Please," Mandy cried as Jess disappeared into the hall, "please don't leave me! PLEASE!"

Jess bolted into the kitchen, scrambling urgently for the cutlery drawer and withdrawing a pair of scratched, rubber-handled scissors. She snapped the blades once and staggered back into the hall, moaning in horror as the music rose and rose, the notes becoming forceful, violent progressions, the highs and lows melting into a thudding storm of music—

"Fuck you!" Jess yelled at nothing in particular as she screamed forward, her heart pounding, only noticing now that the strings were wet with blood, that the carpet was sprayed with it. She lunged forward, splaying her fingers to open the scissors and clamping them around three of the strings.

At once the strings burrowed into Mandy's arm and leg whipped out of her, jetting blood onto the ceiling, and thrust forward into Jess's face. She felt a thick, wet heat spread across her cheeks but couldn't tell where the wires had found purchase, could only feel the searing, sharp sting where the blood fell. She couldn't see. Suddenly everything was black – not just blood running down into her open, screaming mouth but a slick, gelatinous fluid – she couldn't see—

"Jess!" Mandy screamed. Hands on her arms, tears mixing with the blood and the goo of her eyes as the wires snaked deep into her brain. All black, but she felt her whole body rock back as another string smacked into her chest and slithered between her ribs. Another in her throat, like a white-hot injection but the needle kept going and going and going…

More in her throat, digging, exploring. She sunk to her knees, the scissors tumbling from her hand. Something ripped Mandy away from her and she howled in pain and anger and confusion, blind and damp and in so much agony that it was unbearable. "Please," she whispered, "please…"

Something lashed her – hot, sharp, fast – across the neck and she felt warmth spill down her chest. Something else punched through her stomach but she barely felt that at all, just another little tingle of heat.

The last thing she ever heard was the ringing of a seventh chord in her ears.

The music was quiet, calm. Peaceful.

Muffled, it sounded to the neighbours like the same record had been left on repeat, some classical concerto that they must have been too uncultured to recognise. After a while it would grow tedious, but the smell of blood and decaying meat filtering out through the letterbox would give them cause to call the police long before that.

Late on Saturday morning Jess's mobile phone rang in the pocket of her coat. It rang for around eighty seconds, then the caller left a message. The voice seeped through the material of the coat, tinny and muted: "Hi, Jessica, it's Amber. Just wanted to call and see if you're stuck in traffic or something. Nina's getting worried you might have forgotten her! I said no, not your mum, she wouldn't. I hope you're all right, love. Let us know if something's happened, yeah?"

Across the lounge, Mandy whimpered softly into Jess's shoulder. She was exhausted, out of tears, very close to starvation. Or thirst, perhaps. She wondered which would come sooner.

"Please," she whispered, her voice coarse. "Please let me go. Let us go."

The strings coiled around her wrists tightened, their tips buried deep in her tendons. Her fingers worked on something like muscle memory, but the memory was somebody else's. She had never heard the song before.

She tried to scream for help but her mouth was ragged and dry, all the energy sucked out of her. Tried to kick out, to stand up, but the coils of wire round her calves tightened until she couldn't feel her feet.

Jess lay against her, mouth open, eyes punctured and dried on her cheeks. Her throat had been opened up, and the strings that had pierced her chest had driven up into the ceiling of her mouth, slipping between her exposed, bloody vocal cords to create a little cartilage-walled soundbox.

"Please," Mandy whispered as her fingers moved without her permission and she played the cords of her wife's throat. "Let us go. Let us go. Please, dear god…"

Eventually she gave up, closing her eyes and tipping her head back to pray silently for the end. On the stool beside her, a vision of semi-transparent mist in a sharp, grey suit sat and swayed slowly in time with the music, so glad to hear it again, for the first time in so long. He listened with his eyes closed, one hand on her knee, the other gesturing. Conducting.

The music went on long after Mandy's brain had finally shut down, every note an echo of a heartbeat that would never come.

<u>A NOTE FROM THE AUTHOR</u>

Thank you for reading *Dark Nights*. As an independent author every single person reading my work is so valued and I can't express how much your time means to me. For more of my books, follow me on Instagram @heath_horrorwriter or check out my website derekheathhorror.com where I'll keep you updated on future releases.

I hope you enjoyed! If so, please leave a review on Amazon if you can. I'd love to know what you thought.